MATCHED WITH THE BOY NEXT DOOR

ROMANCE BY LOVE, AUSTEN
BOOK 4

BRITNEY M. MILLS

CRYSTAL CANYON PUBLISHING

To Nellie K. Neves
Thank you for the inspiration, the courage, and the amazing light
you give to the book world.

1

EVIE

An hour ago, I was shocked by the chaos that is my roommate's work environment as a nanny. Fifty-nine minutes in and I'm embracing the tornado. Maybe Millie just makes it look like cake, pulling out endless activities and producing snacks out of thin air for her three charges. Maybe she's a trained magician. Or just really good as a future mother.

When she found out her brother was flying in from her hometown in Wyoming this morning, I volunteered as tribute to be the nanny stand-in for a couple hours.

Little did I know that I'm not in shape for kids yet. I mean, I'm the youngest of three and haven't done a whole lot of babysitting in my life. Okay, maybe once. There weren't a lot of opportunities for that. I'd grown up with a nanny and so had most of the people in our neighborhood, so it wasn't like I gained that experience as a typical eleven to fifteen-year-old.

But I love kids and hope that one day I'll find a guy who I can build a life with and have several kids. I've already been through a two-week marriage to someone who married me to avoid marrying the woman his parents picked out for him. When I started having headaches and went temporarily blind, he was done. Been there and I don't want the T-shirt.

The one guy I can count on, I've never seen in person. HuskyHiker521 is my pen pal from a matchmaking app. We don't talk about anything personal, but from all I've learned about him over the past several weeks, I feel like he'd be good with kids.

And we've now gone through most of the activities Millie prepared for the kids this morning.

"Eaty," three-year-old Sarah says, "I want a snack."

I hesitate a moment. The girl has eaten at least three snacks in the last ten minutes. How much is too much when it comes to that kind of thing? No, they're not all sugar filled, but is there a limit to how much I'm supposed to give a child before chaos ensues?

I love children, but I don't know if I was born with the motherly instinct that most women have. Maybe when or if I have my own someday it will all of a sudden click? I'm hoping that's the case.

My resolve crumbles and I open the package of fruit snacks before handing it over to Sarah. "Let's eat it at the table, okay?" There's no argument this time, and I breathe a sigh of relief. This little girl is so darn cute that I have a hard time saying no at all.

A cry through the baby monitor signals that the four-month-old is awake. I hurry into the other room and pick her up, which only makes her cry harder. Her eyes were closed. Does that mean she wasn't quite awake? There is so much to learn and I only have a few of the notes Millie left for me. The girl needs to write a book for those of us with little to no experience in the kid realm.

Five-year-old Devin comes stumbling out of the bathroom. "Can we play a game?"

"Sure. Did you wash your hands?" I ask, knowing that basic hygiene is good no matter how old.

He frowns. "Millie doesn't make me wash my hands."

I mirror his expression. "I live with Millie and she definitely has a thing for germs. Go wash and then we'll play a game."

He lets out a dramatic sigh and walks back toward the bathroom. In that time, I've lost Sarah.

"Sarah! Sarah, where did you go?" I pat the baby's back as I take brisk steps across the house. I check in the kids' bedrooms, which are all bigger than our entire first floor at the Spice House. When Devin comes out of the bathroom, I say, "Where does Sarah hide?"

He rolls his eyes at me, like how dare I, an adult, lose his sister?

He takes a few steps down the hall and waves for me to follow him back to the kitchen. When we round the wall by the island, I see a cubby with what looks like an artist's array of painting supplies. A paint pot is open on the ground, blue paint spilling onto the tile. At least it wasn't on the nearly white carpet. Even I know that color choice is a bad idea with small kids around.

"Sarah, do you want to paint?" I call out, pausing to hear for any rustling. Nothing. I walk over to put the baby in a bouncer and then continue my frenzied search of the house.

Sarah jumps out and says, "Boo!" I stumble back a few steps because I'm jumpy even in the most chill circumstances. With a groan, I take in the sight before me. The girl dumped the red and yellow paints over her head, each color combining so she looks like she's bleeding.

"Devin, will you watch the baby for a minute? I'm going to give Sarah a quick bath."

"She doesn't like baths."

"No water!" Sarah yells and starts to run away. I catch her arm and pull her back gently.

"Okay, how about we wipe you off with some napkins?" Surprisingly, the girl stands like a statue and lets me wipe the paint off. The minute I get a napkin wet, though, she runs out of the room and hides again. At least I saw her departure this time and can follow to the same room.

It's a struggle, but I set her in the clawfoot tub and use the sprayer to get the paint off completely. It looks like it might've been finger paints and the washable kind, thank goodness. I'll have to thank Millie a dozen times that it wasn't something that would stain. Her bosses are already very strict, from all the stories I've heard, and I don't want to make things worse for her.

After a change into dry clothes, Sarah takes off again. I move the paints to a higher shelf and glance around, hoping that we won't have a similar situation in another five minutes.

"Can we play Twister?" Devin asks, holding a box out.

I nod, trying to regain some of the upbeat attitude I had when I first arrived. One thing I've learned in this short time is that kids can smell the fear.

Devin hops over to the living room and lays out the mat, placing the spinner on the table. The baby has gone back to sleep so I walk over and pick up the spinner board.

"Okay, the first one is... right hand red."

"You have to do it too," Devin says.

I grimace, knowing that my flexibility skills are almost nonexistent. Most young girls were put into ballet or some kind of dance class. After my mother died when I was young, my father was in charge of the activities. My extracurriculars consisted of piano lessons twice a week and sewing lessons. So, I can play a sonata or sew a dress but touching my toes is another story.

Millie should be back soon. I can handle a few minutes of what is basically a glorified ab plank game. I lean over and put my right hand on red on the edge of the mat.

Devin spins. Left leg on blue, which is right next to the red. Not bad. This is doable.

Another spin has our left hand on blue as well. Devin spins a fourth time and it's right leg on green, which is on the other side of the mat. I have to think through how to get everything on the right spots without removing my already planted limbs. I twist my left leg, trying to get even a toe from my right foot on one of the green circles. Instead, my left foot gets stuck on the plastic surface and I hear something crack before a jolt of pain attacks my foot.

I end up landing on my side on the mat.

"You lose! I am the ultimate winner!" Devin says, doing a victory dance next to me.

"You did great," I say through clenched teeth. As much as I'd like to say I have a high-pain tolerance, that would be a lie. I'm a total wuss and have to use all my extra energy to not let the tears escape.

The smallest movement steals my breath away. The pain starts near my pinky toe and travels down toward the middle of the top of my foot. Sitting on the floor isn't helping things either. I press up on my hands and manage to stand on one foot. I'm a flamingo as I hop toward the couch with my injured foot tucked under me. Of course, the couch is a modern one and it feels as though I'm sitting on a wooden chair, but the relief is worth it.

"Let's play again," Devin says, his voice a bit louder than a few seconds ago.

"Jenny is still asleep, Devin," I manage to say. "How about we watch a show for a bit?" Ten minutes ago, I would've shunned the idea to stick him in front of a screen, but I need a few minutes to regroup here.

"Millie never lets us watch shows during the day."

As much as I want to balk at that statement, I'm just glad this isn't my full-time job. "Well, think of this as a treat."

He grabs the controller and turns on the TV, which causes Sarah to appear out of nowhere. She sits down and it's probably the quietest it's been since I arrived sixty-eight minutes ago.

I put my feet on the coffee table, going against every rule I was ever taught when it comes to decorum. But I'm in pain and trying to figure out what to do. Ice should be involved in this injury. Ibuprofen as well. If only I was at home right now to find everything where I know it will be.

My brain turns to HuskyHiker521. What would he say about my injury? Probably something like I wouldn't be able to join him in the great outdoors for a while. The guy is always recommending local trails for beautiful scenery.

We've only been chatting about a month through a forum in the Love, Austen app. The top rule we made with each other for our pen-pal-ship was that we wouldn't give too many real-life particulars. I don't know if it's the anonymity that makes me excited when I receive a message from him, or that I'm talking to a male without the pressure of what's supposed to come next.

All my roommates have used the app at some point in the last few months. I was avoiding being matched with anyone and stumbled into the forum area, a little like Reddit but not as extensive. HuskyHiker521 and I bonded over traveling, something I did a lot as a kid with my dad and two brothers.

I try to recall what he said last, something about wanting to travel to Europe at some point. Munich and Berlin are my votes for him to visit first. Rich history, the people, the food, the Eisbach in the summer. It's basically a river running through the city of Munich. My brothers, Luke and Drew, and I spent a lot of time there, enjoying the cool water in the middle of the hot summer.

HuskyHiker521 has given me several places to hit in New England alone. I'd been planning to visit a trail he said is starting to bloom with the change of leaves this coming weekend. From the pain in my foot, I'm going to have to delay that a bit.

Another fifteen minutes pass and the door opens. A wall obstructs us from the opening, but I'm hoping it's Millie and not her bosses.

"Evie! We're back. Where are you?" Millie's voice calls.

"We're in the living room." I feel like I've become part of this awful couch in the past dozen minutes, which means I must be hurting.

Millie shows up around the corner, as does a man. He looks a lot like her, although his hair is more of a sandy brown than the auburn of Millie's.

"This is my brother, Beau. Beau, this is Evie. She's one of my roommates."

I nod, forcing a smile despite the pain. "It's so nice to meet you. Millie said you're here for work?"

Beau smiles and says, "Yeah. One of my really good friends from college lives here and we've been working on some ideas for a production company."

Millie glances down at my foot and says, "What happened?"

"Twister happened." That's all I can say before I start laughing. Getting injured playing that game never even occurred to me.

"Your foot is a little swollen. Let me get you some ice." Millie disappears and comes back within seconds. It probably would've taken me at least five minutes to locate a baggy, ten with me hopping like a bunny. "How did things go here?"

"We're watching a show," Devin says with a devilish grin.

Millie nods. "I see that. I guess there won't be TV time this afternoon. We'll just have to stare at the walls."

Devin's eyes go wide and he quickly turns off the TV. "We didn't watch it that long. Can I please watch Dog Patrollers?"

Millie gives him a look like she's negotiating with some high-powered attorney and then her face softens for a moment. "If you make sure your bed is made and your chores are done, I think we can watch that new episode you've been waiting for."

Devin jumps up and whoops. And then he's gone, running down the hall toward the bedrooms.

"How do you do that?" I ask, shaking my head. It's almost like she's the Good Witch from The Wizard of Oz and just waved her wand to get him to react. I need to invest in a notebook to write all this down for the future.

Millie laughs and Beau chuckles behind her. "We had some strict parents growing up. I'm trying to strike a balance between extreme and too lenient, which is sometimes what happens with their parents. And I've been working here for the past eight months, so we've made a lot of progress."

My phone pings and I see it's a text from Judy, my boss at Bridal Oasis.

Judy: *Where are you? We've got several appointments today that need to be a success.*

I glance up and say, "Well, I better get going. The Queen has already questioned my tardiness, even though I told her I'd be coming in late today."

"Thank you so much for helping me out, Evie," Millie says.

"I'm just glad you arrived when you did," I say, laughing. I push off the couch and try to put weight on my foot but it buckles below me, causing me to stumble. I catch myself against the wall and try to smile at Millie and her brother.

I've got at least a ten-hour shift in my future, which involves a lot of walking back and forth, carrying wedding dresses into dressing rooms. This is not a good sign.

"Are you all right?" Beau asks.

"I think I sprained something in my foot. I don't have time to be off it today." Of all the days to have injured my foot, this was not the best option. Judy is already riled up that our sales numbers are down, but I'm doing what I can to help out, even taking over the tailoring since the last seamstress left for another company a few weeks ago.

Millie's eyes go wide and she says, "I think I have something you can use for today at least."

She again disappears and then comes back like she apparated in front of me holding an Ace bandage.

"It's not as strong as a foot brace, but maybe it will help until you can get it checked out. Actually, you might want to go get looked at now."

"I'll be fine. It's probably just a sprained toe and you know how little I deal with pain. I'll just ice it and wait for the swelling to go down."

This could work.

"Thank you so much." I sit back down and wrap the

bandage around my foot and up around my ankle. The pressure of the bandage helps ease some of the pain. Until I stand. "That will work," I eke out, trying to edge the corners of my mouth upward.

"How are you getting to work?" Millie asks.

"Walking and the train. I'll be fine."

Millie shakes her head. "No, I'll have Beau drive you there. Then I can get the kids back on their routine before the afternoon chaos hits."

Beau nods and takes the keys from Millie. "As long as you know where to go, I'll get you there."

I'm grateful to not have to fight crowds this morning while hoping no one will accidentally step on my foot. That is until I realize Millie's awful driving skills must be hereditary. She'd volunteered to drive the roommates out to the mud run our roommate, Kenzie, made us sign up for a couple weeks ago and we were all in danger of whiplash on that excursion. I'd always assumed that driving differed with each person, but it seems like the brake tapping dance is genetic with the Larsen family.

By the time I arrive at Bridal Oasis, a bridal boutique I've been working at for the past seven months, not only do I have pain in my foot, but also my head and neck. I thank Beau for the ride and breathe a sigh of relief that I'm on solid ground and I can control my own fate. I've had too many close calls lately.

"You're finally here," Judy says through gritted teeth as I hurry into the employee room. I have to limp/run as I go, doing my best to keep the pain from becoming audible. I swallow a couple ibuprofen I keep in my cubby in back and head out onto the floor.

From babysitter to bridal consultant, this day couldn't get any more strange.

2

OWEN

Working as an ER nurse on the night shift, getting to sleep each day is a process, one that involves blackout shades and a sound machine. I'm like a twenty-eight-year-old newborn, unable to sleep through the night.

It hasn't been like this forever, though. I mean, just a few weeks ago, I was dating the love of my life with plans for our future. Now I feel like the curmudgeon on *Up*. Maybe I need to get a dog or find a Wilderness troop to volunteer for and embrace the grump completely.

Something is shaking me and it takes several moments for me to realize it's not part of my dream. Opening one eye, I see my friend, Jack.

"Didn't anyone teach you to knock?" I ask, rolling over so I'm not facing him. For once I didn't jump at the surprise of seeing someone there. I must be extra tired this morning. Or afternoon. I haven't seen a clock for a while.

"Yeah, I did that for at least five minutes. Luckily you haven't switched where you keep your spare key under the fire extinguisher. I had to make sure you weren't dead since no one has heard from you in a few days. Get up."

Shaking my head, I say, "No. I'm not on shift until tonight."

"It's tonight already. Don't you have to be at the hospital at six?"

I jerk awake, focusing my eyes so they finally see the time on the alarm clock next to me. 5:04 pm. Throwing the covers back, I hurry out of bed and into the bathroom. It's only when my brain clears that I realize Jack is still here.

I put on a cleanish set of scrubs and splash water on my face. "What brings you here, Jack? Did you run out of animals to wrangle?"

We've been friends for years, and when he announced that he was going to vet school, our friend group was all shocked. He gives off the slacker vibe usually, but he was in the top 1% of his graduating class, and he's increased the business they've had at the vet clinic he's been working at for the past two years.

"No, that's why I'm here," he says with a wide grin.

"I'm not an animal," I say, glancing up at the face in the mirror. My hair is matted on one side and my eyes are slightly bloodshot from the lack of sleep I've gotten lately. The nap Jack woke me from was probably the best sleep I've had in weeks.

"That is yet to be determined." Jack's smile disappears into his neutral expression. The guy is usually teasing someone to death and this sober expression means something is off.

"Why did you really come? And how did you know what time my shift starts?" I ask, turning to face him completely.

"Me and the guys, we're worried about you, man. You don't need to get fired because of heartbreak."

That comment slices right through me. Sure, it's been rough ever since I came back from a humanitarian medical mission to Central America. Riley was supposed to come with me but she wasn't cleared because of the flu. I leave for a month and come back to find out she's moved on with one of the resident doctors at the hospital. I cringe to think that I'd picked out a ring and had planned to propose a week or two later.

"I'm not going to get fired," I say, brushing past him to grab a pair of socks out of the drawer.

"The guys are planning to go rowing on the Charles tomorrow. You in?"

I look at him dryly. "What time? I won't be home until six in the morning."

"We're meeting up at six-thirty. Think you can hold off sleeping a bit longer and hang out with us?"

I shrug and focus on putting on my socks. "I'll let you know tomorrow."

"If you don't go there, maybe we can hit up a movie later. Spencer is working with his business partner most of the next week, so I'm free whenever."

I shake my head. "Great, I've become a Spencer stand-in." I bite my tongue and sigh. I sound more bitter than I wanted to. "Sorry, I didn't mean it like that."

"Good, because Spencer and I do a lot together, but that doesn't mean you're a backup. We're all worried about you, man. We just want you to be happy."

That's easy enough to say. Miles and Trey are over the moon with their significant others and even the newest addition to the group, Landon, seems like life is so great because he's married. I don't know if that will be in the cards for me now. I've lost a lot in the past year from the death of my mother and breaking up with Riley. Maybe I'll see things differently in a couple weeks, but I doubt it.

"Thanks, Jack. I appreciate it, man. But right now, I've got to jet so I can make it to the hospital." As I grab my backpack and load it with whatever is easily edible for my midnight dinner break, I let his words swirl around in my brain. "You know, we can be happy without a woman by our side, right?"

Jack frowns. "Where did that come from?"

"I'm just saying, I know that the past few weeks have been rough, but I'm still happy. I don't need a woman to complete me."

That's when the frown turns upside down. "Wow, are you sure about that? Is this one of the steps on the grief staircase? The Owen I know was whipped from the moment he started dating Riley. And you say you're okay without her. I call bull."

"I'm living, breathing, smiling," I say, trying to emphasize my fake smile. "I have a great, steady job and time to go see all the places I want when I want. There's no lie about that."

"You're also Mr. Tidy and look at this place," Jack says, sweeping his arms wide to take in the room. I glance around, seeing for the first time in at least two weeks what my apartment looks like. I don't know if I had blinders on, but I'm disgusted.

Takeout containers and soda cans are on almost every surface. I hardly drink anything but water normally. The sink is full of dishes that have crusts on them, and if I had a goldfish, the bowl would probably be slimy at this point.

"Maybe I wanted to be more like you, Jack," I say, laughing as I turn the knob to the front door.

"I doubt that. Plan on it tomorrow, all right? If you don't

come row on the Charles with us, I'll come here in the afternoon to get you after you've had your nap."

I shrug. "We'll see how I'm feeling tomorrow." A noncommittal answer is an answer, at least I hope Jack will buy it.

"You need to get back to dating."

Shaking my head, I say, "Trey said something about Hillary being one of Kenzie's roommates. Weren't you two close a while back?" It's something I've been wanting to ask Jack since I met Hillary with Kenzie a week ago.

His face turns to stone. "Ancient history, man. You better head out. You'll be late."

"You're going to have to talk about this at some point, man," I say, smiling as I grab my keys from the counter.

"You too, O. I promise not to tease you if you need to chat."

I turn to study his face. There's no malice, no hint of teasing in his expression. "I promise, I'm fine. I'm working through things one day at a time. I've even been using that dumb app everyone in our group is using."

Jack doesn't get surprised easily and now his eyebrows are practically lifting off his face. "You're on the app? Did you get matched?"

Now's the part where I have to decide how much to tell him. If I say that I've got a platonic pen pal, he might never leave me alone about dating. But I'm strong enough to handle it. I've made it this far.

"I haven't been matched, but I've been exploring several areas of the app. Maybe in a few months I'll get back on the proverbial horse."

Jack slaps me on the back. "That's all any of us can do, man."

We head out of the building and say goodbye.

I'm on the train and open the Love, Austen app. I'd written a response to TheWeddingPlanner2's message this morning before falling asleep after work. We've been communicating for the past couple weeks and since there is no pressure about "where the relationship is going," it's been easy to open up about random topics.

She's a world traveler and I've been impressed by her suggestions of places to visit so far. My only claim to travel outside the continental U.S. was a few weeks ago to Guatemala.

I read through what I sent her this morning, wishing I'd used spell check or something since in my tired state, I misspelled two words.

To: HuskyHiker521

From: TheWeddingPlanner2

Am I a wedding planner because of my screenname? No, I'm not a wedding planner. I figured that putting WeddingPlanner as a handle might scare away some of the more serious candidates.

I'M NOT ready for a relationship yet but was looking for a pen pal and I'm so grateful we've been able to connect about travel destinations. It's been a while since I've gone anywhere.

I'LL PUT that trail on my list for the upcoming weeks.

ARE you into dressing up for Halloween?

. . .

I SMILE and think about the last time I dressed up for Halloween. Probably my first year of college when the guys and I went to a party dressed as various characters from Super Mario. I ended up as Bowser, since I'm taller and broader than the rest. Jack was Mario and Spencer dressed as Luigi, the tall green brother. I can't remember what characters Miles and Trey went as, but we got a ton of compliments on the coordination.

I settle in to write her back. Maybe it's just my brain, but it's like a boost of serotonin every time I see a message from her.

To: TheWeddingPlanner2
   From: HuskyHiker521

IT'S BEEN *a while since I've dressed up for Halloween. What about you? Have you been planning your costume since January?* ☺

   Life has been interesting lately. I'm trying to decide if I should change jobs in the future. I like the one I have, there are just a lot of memories that haunt me now.

   If you can get out and see that trail, or even the one at Mt. Auburn Cemetery, the leaves make the trees look like they're on fire. It's one of my favorite things about fall.

THE HIKE I took earlier this week was amazing with the small pops of red, yellow and orange on the trees. There's a slight longing to have someone there with me to walk through and take in the beautiful landscape. But then I remember the humiliation of showing up at Riley's door after my trip to find another guy answering the door with a soda in his hand.

Trust isn't something I'm in great supply of right now, so I'll just venture out and admire the landscape myself. I can always invite my sister, Darcy, and her fiancé. They're so busy with wedding preparations that it would be hard to get away. And I'd be the third wheel once again.

Inviting the guys to go would mean I'd get bombarded with questions on how I'm doing and how they can help every five minutes. Maybe I need to book a trip to a beach and hang out for a week to reset my brain.

I get off the train and walk into the hospital. A trip might be the best option to help me concentrate on something other than the breakup. Maybe TheWeddingPlanner2 will have an idea of somewhere a bit closer.

3

EVIE

Longest day of my life. I can feel the exhaustion through every cell of my body and my ibuprofen has worn off because my foot is throbbing with pain.

The reward for going into work today was that six of my appointments found the dress of their dreams. That's been my goal ever since I became a wedding dress consultant—to make sure that every woman found a dress they love so they don't have to go to so many different shops. The only gal who didn't decide on a dress said she wanted to bring a couple more friends back to help her decide.

I hobble into the house just before dark after a nine-hour shift and sink onto the bottom stair that leads to the second level, trying to decide if I should head up there and curl up on the couch for a few hours or if I should just go to bed.

I check my messages again. HuskyHiker usually responds quickly in the evenings. I already read his last message during my break at work, but didn't have a chance to write back until after we closed at eight. My foot was throbbing so much, I'd taken a few seconds to sit down and order an Uber and had been able to respond while waiting for it to arrive.

The front door opens, and my roommate Hillary walks in. "Hey, what's up?" she asks.

"Just resting after a long day. What have you been up to?" I grin as I take in her appearance in a large blue ball gown.

"Oh, you know, just got done playing Cinderella." She sits down on the step next to me, her dress billowing out around her, and sighs. "It's nice that it's so quiet here. The mother of the birthday kid had invited thirty five-year-olds to the party. She brought in reinforcements, but still. That's a lot of energy all in one room."

I laugh, thinking about how I'd said the same thing this morning. "I feel that. Going from three kids under the age of five to dress hunting for women who might be emotionally around that age has me feeling like a melted piece of cheese."

"Melted cheese is the best part though."

I laugh, which feels good after the events of today. Leave it to Hillary to help me break up the exhaustion and pain coursing through my body. Slipping off my shoe, I undo the Ace bandage and breathe out. To be honest, I feel little relief with it off and there's an imprint where my foot swelled by the edge of the shoe.

"What happened to your foot?" Hillary asks, pointing.

"I think I sprained my toe playing Twister?" I don't know why I say it as a question.

"And you walked all over with it today?"

I'm usually practical, always taking public transportation to get anywhere since it's a lot cheaper than paying for a cab, but after the day I've had, I caved. "Millie's brother took me to work and I took an Uber home. There was no way I could even walk from the shop to the T station, let alone make it through all the transfers to get home."

She leans over to touch my foot and I pull it away. "What are you doing?"

"I was just going to see if it's sprained or broken." Hillary looks at me like that should be a standard response to a hurt foot.

"How would you know?"

Hillary shakes her head. "I was a lifeguard in high school and took a few medical classes."

That makes me feel even worse. A year ago, I was on track to become a full-fledged nurse, but couldn't finish because of my health, and I can't tell whether my foot is broken? Then again, the pain has been blinding a lot of what I've felt today.

I reach over and probe, wincing with each touch.

"It's broken, isn't it?"

I groan. "I don't think I'll know without an x-ray."

"I'll change and then drive you to the ER."

Shaking my head, I say, "I'll just take some medicine and go to sleep. We'll know in the morning."

"You'll also have to work and the more you walk around without finding out what's wrong could make it worse. What if it heals funny?"

I'm not sure how to take this. I'm usually the one looking into the future in this house, making sure all the roomies are taking care of themselves. Having Hillary, of all the room-mates, take over that role feels like I made some sort of time warp jump into another dimension.

"Fine. I still think it will be fine tomorrow without anything. You can drive, but I don't want to hear an 'I-told-you-so' after, all right?" I try to give her a stern look, but with her dressed as a princess, it's hard to keep a straight face.

Hillary laughs. "I can't promise anything." She turns and jets up the stairs. I sit on the bottom step, wishing I didn't have the constant throb of pain in my foot.

Moving into this house was the best thing that ever happened to me, keeping me afloat when my life had imploded not long before. Having a roommate who's willing to drop everything and drive me to the hospital means more than I could've asked for.

Todd, my ex-husband, would've told me to "suck it up and get through it." We only made it two weeks as a married couple, and I can't imagine what life would be like if we hadn't gotten the marriage annulled. Pushing through can be true of some situations, but from how the pain in my foot has only increased, all the warning bells are going off in my head that I need to get this checked out.

Hillary comes down in a pair of sweats and a t-shirt, a jacket over her arm. The joy of Boston in the fall is the humidity can make it sweltering in the day but also cold at night.

"Let's do this."

The drive to the hospital isn't long. The good part is that on a Thursday night, not too many people are blocking the roads to get to Mass Health Hospital. And because every other entrance is closed for the night, we have to stop at the ER.

"This is going to be rough on my insurance," I say.

"Are you not on your parents' insurance?" Hillary asks.

I shake my head. "My dad loves to make sure we can take care of ourselves." I'm actually grateful for that, because I grew up knowing the value of money when several of my cousins didn't quite get that. They've blown through their trust funds in just a few short years.

"Well, you've got a job. At least it will help pay for some of it." Hillary gets out of the car and walks over to where I'm standing. "Maybe you should sue Millie's bosses."

I raise an eyebrow. "For being a klutz and twisting my toe while watching their kids? They don't even know Millie left for the airport. That's not even an option, Hill."

I lean onto Hillary as we walk in, feeling bad that most of my weight is pulling down on her shoulder. Even trying to put my foot down the littlest bit would probably cause me to fall over onto the ground at this point. After limping all day, I'm not sure why it's suddenly so much harder to get around. Maybe it's because I don't have anything to distract me from the pain right now.

We make it inside and a nurse glances up. She takes all my information and disappears to the back somewhere. There are at least five other people waiting, and I'm not excited about spending most of the night here. Not that I've been here much for myself, but I spent a fair amount of time in the hospital when my dad had to be admitted for a heart attack and then again for pneumonia.

Positive thoughts. I need to think of something good that came from this. At least Hillary was home to bring me in. As much as I try to be independent, there are some situations that are much easier with someone by my side.

"Thank you for bringing me in," I say, giving Hillary a smile.

"No problem. It's never fun seeing you in pain, Evie." She leans over and gives my shoulder a squeeze.

Hillary helps me sit down in a chair before she opens up one of the magazines on a table in front of us. I try to focus on the TV in the corner, which is featuring a rerun of one of the older sitcoms my dad used to watch, but the pain is getting worse.

I finally sit back in the seat and close my eyes. This isn't the best place to fall asleep, but I'm exhausted from the day and I need to relax so my brain won't be hyper focused on my foot.

I open an eye when I feel someone shaking my shoulder. Hillary's face comes into view. "Evie, Kenzie and Millie are here."

"Okay," I say, yawning. "Wait, what?" I glance up to see my other two roommates standing behind her.

"Rachelle is having some complications with her pregnancy. I need to go be with her for some sisterly support. I guess it's something about the placenta being out of place. I need to go be with her, but I didn't want you to be alone so I called in reinforcements."

How long had I been asleep? I glance at the clock on the wall and see it's midnight. Two hours and I didn't hear a thing. I must've been tired.

"Go," I say, "Make sure that baby is okay." Rachelle and Landon were the first in our friend group to get married several months ago. They were worried they wouldn't be able to have kids because of health concerns but ended up getting pregnant on their honeymoon.

Millie and Kenzie settle in next to me. "You two don't have to be here," I say, shifting my body to the side so I can lean on the armrest. I'm in the groggy state of having too long of a nap and not wanting to wake up completely.

"You're here because of me," Millie says, leaning in for a quick hug.

"It's not because of you. It was a freak accident."

"Well, roommates stick together," Kenzie says, giving me a tired smile. Her days are split among her work as an organizer, her boyfriend Trey, and her love of hockey. No wonder she's tired.

I blow out a breath and lean over to take Millie's hand. "Thank you. To be honest, I'm nervous and very happy to have you both here."

Nervous is an understatement. Now that I'm awake, I think about all the things that are behind the ER doors. All the smells of antiseptic and bleach. I'd wanted to be a nurse for so long. Quitting nursing school when I was so close to finishing was the hardest thing I've done. But the stress was too much. I haven't been in a hospital since then.

"Evelyn Evans." I glance up to the door and sigh with relief that maybe I can get a break from all this. Even a few minutes of pain relief is welcome right now.

"That's you, Evie," Millie says, as if I didn't hear already. She's on one side and Kenzie on the other, helping me get up. But instead of me leaning on them, a male nurse comes in with a wheelchair. He's tall with broad shoulders and a slight wave to his blond hair. He's got eyes that look like the sea. He'd make a good male model.

"You can have a seat here," he says, but his voice is almost bored.

"Owen? I didn't know you were working tonight," Kenzie says.

I glance between the nurse and Kenzie, wondering what the connection is. Kenzie didn't have a ton of ex-boyfriends before she and Trey got together, but there's a lot of her past I don't know about still. It wasn't until a few months after living under the same roof that she admitted to us about having a crush on Trey since she was in youth hockey.

The nurse gives her a surprised smile and says, "I didn't think I'd see you tonight, Kenzie. What did you break this time?" Did he not see that she's walking just fine while I look like I'm walking a tightrope?

Kenzie shakes her head. "Believe it or not, we're not here for me. Evie is my roommate." She points to me and for some reason the heat creeps up my neck with embarrassment. I'm going to have to explain what happened to this guy, who Kenzie knows, and I'm never going to live this down.

Once I'm in the wheelchair, I slink down. I didn't realize it would be this hard to get places when my foot is out of order.

"Foot injury?" Nurse Owen asks.

"Yes," is all I can say. I'm beyond niceties right now. I need to elevate my foot and get some more pain medicine in me before I can think clearly. There are people who get angry when they're hungry, and people call it hangry. I get angry when I'm in pain so I'd call it pangry. That's right. I'm going to make that one a trend.

He turns the wheelchair around and steers me through the door and down the hallway. We enter a room to the left. It's extra bright with the luminescent bulbs and the smell of cleaner. He stops the wheelchair and stands a foot away. "Have a seat on the bed while I pull up your chart."

I go to stand but am intercepted by two pairs of hands digging into my armpits as they lift. "I didn't break my spine," I say, chuckling a bit.

"We don't want to make your injury worse," Kenzie says, acting as though lifting me is no big deal. "Isn't that part of your job, Owen? She is injured."

I freeze and turn to look at him. She must be close to him to give him a hard time like that.

Owen puts down the papers in his hand and walks over, lifting me under the armpits and planting me onto the bed.

He lifts me like he's lifting a book. I'm surprised that he smells good, but when I see his pinched lips, I know it's better to just stay far away.

"Smooth, Owen," Kenzie says, shaking her head. "What's got your boxers in a twist?"

His eyes flash at her words. Kenzie glances from his face to mine and back. "Too similar?"

He only gives a curt nod and goes back to the computer.

Did I get the grumpy nurse? Or did I already do something to tick him off? I'm too tired to worry about making him like me. I need several pain killers and a dark room for at least three days to recover from the pain.

Time to redirect my focus. I motion to Kenzie and try to mouth, "How do you know him?"

Kenzie gives me a sly smile and says, "Owen, Trey was telling me the guys are rowing on the Charles tomorrow morning. Are you going?"

Owen turns and gives her a look that says he's not amused. "Is Trey making you needle me into going? I already got the third degree from Jack right before my shift today."

"Wait, you know Trey and Jack?" I say without thinking.

He turns to give me a quick look before he focuses back on the screen. "Yeah, Jack and Spencer, Trey and Miles. And some new guy named Landon who's pretty cool. We've been doing stuff for years. Mostly getting each other out of sticky situations."

"We've hung out with all the guys a lot. I don't remember you from the mud run," I say, my mind spinning a wheel. Then again, if Kenzie knows who he is, he must be telling the truth.

Owen sighs and taps one more key with more force than the rest. "Probably because I was traveling home from a medical mission. I need to make sure these stats are correct, so I've got a list of questions for you." For the next five minutes, he goes over my entire medical history. His voice sounds like he's either falling asleep standing up or he's extra bored and would rather be anywhere but here. The one part he doesn't ask about was the stint at the end of nursing school when I had a stress breakdown. I'm kind of glad that's not in the file yet.

Next up are the vitals, which means he's awfully close to me. At least he smells good, a mix of pine and leather.

"Okay," he says, pushing the keyboard tray in and walking over to sit on the stool. "We'll need to remove the bandage." He starts unwrapping the bandage. Millie and Kenzie are so quiet, it's almost unnerving, like we're being spied on by statues or something.

There are indentations from the bandage, the rest of my foot is swollen with a few hints of black and blue bruising.

"Can you tell me what happened?" Grumpy Owen says.

I can't see his face but the humiliation settles inside me once again. "I, uh, think I might've sprained my toe this morning." I don't know if the half-truth or the whole-truth sounds worse.

"What is your usual pain level?" he asks.

"Well, I usually can handle more than this," I say, with a chuckle. That might be a stretch.

He just makes a sound like he doesn't believe that.

"Having hobbled around most of the day, I'd say I gave it the old college try to get over the pain." My words have more bite than normal. Either Kenzie is rubbing off on me or I really can't handle pain.

He touches the area a bit and I wince, doing my best to be brave almost to spite him. I have a thing about feet in general, people touching my feet or someone else's feet in my vicinity. The fact I didn't rear back and kick him is a miracle.

Grumpy Owen slides back over to the computer and taps away at the keyboard again. It seems like he'll never stop, so I shift back and lean against the upright portion of the bed.

"Okay, I've ordered an x-ray. We'll come get you when we're ready for it."

He walks out the door and it's like we've been holding our breath for the last few minutes. Okay, maybe it was just me.

"He's friends with the guys?" I ask, looking at Kenzie.

She shrugs. "Yeah, he's a pretty great guy. Things haven't been going well for him lately and the guys are kind of worried about him. His girlfriend dumped him right after he got back from his trip. Trey said he was ready to propose."

Grumpy Nurse was in a relationship long enough to consider proposing? That's something my brain can't wrap itself around.

"Why is he mad at me then?"

Kenzie gives me a pained smile. "You look similar to his ex and have the same color hair."

"Have you met her?"

"Once," Kenzie says. "Owen had to drop some stuff off to her and Trey and I were with him. She's a piece of work."

"I think Spencer told me about him at one of our get-togethers," Millie says. She looks as though she's trying to keep her eyes open.

It's strange, but I usually go out of my way to get to know people, but I'm way behind on whoever Ornery Owen is.

The x-ray takes a few minutes, only hurting for a few seconds as they had to get multiple angles of my foot. I'm brought back to the same room to find Millie snoring softly in her chair and Kenzie looking at something on her phone.

After several minutes, there's finally a knock on the door and I shift to look more awake, having started to drift off.

"Hello, Ms. Evans," the doctor says, giving me a nod as he walks in. "Why don't you tell me about your injury?"

I open my mouth to speak and realize Grumpy Nurse Owen is standing in the corner. Why was I willing to spill my story with no reservations when I thought he wasn't in the room?

Deep breath, Evie.

"I was tending the kids that my roommate, Millie, nannies for this morning." I point to her sitting in the chair next to the bed. "It was kind of chaotic and the little boy wanted to play Twister, like the game with the mat and the colored dots."

The doctor smiles. "I'm familiar with it."

"Anyway, after several moves, I twisted my foot and ended up getting my toe stuck one way while the rest of my foot went another."

Laughter comes from the corner and I do my best to channel Hillary's glare, which actually works enough to get Nurse Owen to stop.

The doctor prods my foot a little and with each touch, I'm wincing. "Okay, let's check out this x-ray."

Why didn't he do that in the first place? I'm getting more and more irritated with pain and my patience is nearly empty. Breathe, Evie.

The doctor smiles and walks over to the computer, tapping away. When he puts the sheets up on the wall with the light behind it, I gasp. There are at least two places where the bones aren't connected.

"Is it broken?" I ask, even though I can see the answer.

He turns and nods to me. "It looks like when your pinky toe got stuck on the mat, it pulled and ended up breaking these two bones right here. The good news is that the bones haven't chipped off and didn't move much. We'll put your foot in a boot for six to eight weeks to help it heal. You can also make an appointment with the orthopedic surgeon, just to make sure there's no lasting damage. He might leave you in the splint or cast it, depending on how it looks when the swelling goes down." He glances up and his expression changes. "Are you doing okay?"

I nod, trying to clear my mind as I think of all the things swirling through me. Laughter bubbles up in my throat and I shake my head as I say, "I just can't believe this happened playing Twister."

The doctor laughs with me. "This is definitely a new one." His phone buzzes and after a quick glance he turns to Grumpy Owen and says, "Will you get her set up and then come help? There's been a pileup. The ER is about to get busy."

That's not what I want to happen. The doctor says goodbye and disappears out the door. He must've taken all the air with him because once Grumpy Owen comes into view, it's way too hot and stuffy in here.

He doesn't say anything, and I'm wishing I could be anywhere else right now. I usually don't have a problem making friends with just about anyone, and yet this guy seems annoyed by my presence. A normal person would laugh with me about my misfortune. This guy seems to be a grump all around. Then again, he did smile and laugh earlier, so maybe he's not a complete robot.

"How long will this take?" I ask, shifting in the bed to get in a better position.

"Why? Are you missing a date because of it?"

The sneer on the man's face as he sits on the small rolling stool has me blowing out air so I don't say something I don't mean.

"Believe it or not, people have to work for a living. I'm sure you understand some part of that. I'd rather not be out of a job tomorrow." On the scale of tiredness, I'm at a fifteen.

"You sure you'll be able to go to work with an injured foot? Where do you work?"

Letting out a long breath, I say, "I'll be able to work." Although getting around with a broken foot is going to be a challenge.

"She's one of the best at picking out–" Millie starts.

"Flowers," I say, not wanting him to know anything more about me. Chances are high I'll have to see him again at some point, especially since he's friends with all my friends' significant others. But I've gotten strange comments when people find out I help women find their wedding dress. Things like I won't get married because guys will think I'm gunning to get hitched from the first date. Not that dating this guy is even an option.

Kenzie and Millie look at me like I've morphed into some kind of alien, but I'm tired, ornery, and ready to go to sleep.

Grumpy Owen fits me with a small boot that fits up to just above my ankle. "Crutches or scooter?"

I shake my head, trying to figure out what he means when it finally dawns on me. "Scooter," I say, my voice resigned. If I'm clumsy walking normally, I don't need the crutches sliding out from underneath me and breaking the other foot.

"I'll have someone bring it in, along with your discharge paperwork." With that, he leaves. "Good to see you, Kenzie."

"Thank you, Mr. No Bedside Manner," I murmur once he's gone.

Kenzie bursts out laughing. "I can't believe you just said that."

"I blame you for my sarcastic tongue under duress," I say, grinning at her. "I'm ready to go home. At least this boot is helping with some of the pain. I just hope the doctor gives me a pain prescription. I don't think ibuprofen is going to cut it for a few days."

At least there's some relief in sight. Maybe I can get home and get some sleep.

I'll worry about getting around tomorrow. And seeing the jerk at the next friend get together.

4

OWEN

It's been a long week. Like, unbearably long. Riley dumped me eighty-seven days ago and no, I haven't counted that down to the minutes and seconds. Although having Kenzie's roommate as a patient brought up way too much resentment from my breakup. Evelyn Evans doesn't look exactly like Riley, but her look and mannerisms just brought out the worst in me.

After a night of dealing with the victims of the pileup, I can't do much of anything, especially while not thinking clearly.

So many people were wounded, but only one death for a woman in her seventies. It's hard to see anyway, but I've been volunteering at a senior rehabilitation center since I got back from Guatemala. Several of the people that I visit there have become like family. I'm sure it would be hard to see any of them in the same position.

For some reason, my brain keeps recalling Twister-girl, probably to get over reliving all the trauma from the night. She is definitely feisty, and I wonder why I can't just turn off my mind and go to sleep. Probably because there's something about her that I can't quite figure out. Maybe the fact that she wasn't automatically swooning in front of me?

That sounds arrogant, but I've gotten several numbers just by treating patients. Not that I've ever used any of them. I was so gone for and in love with Riley that I didn't think about any other women. I wish she could say the same about me.

I search for a message from TheWeddingPlanner2, hoping her words will have some effect on my mind and allow me to finally fall asleep.

Nothing.

My heart sinks a bit. There's something about this pen-pal-ship that is helping ease my own pain. I can talk to the guys about certain things, but not everything. At the rate we're going, TheWeddingPlanner2 and I might know each other better than anyone else because of some real conversations we've had. I have no fear of her making fun of me, which I can take about any topic but my mother's death and Riley's betrayal.

I finally get home around nine-thirty in the morning, having stayed longer than my shift to help with the burden of patients.

My phone rings and it's my sister.

"Hey Darcy," I say, picking up the call. I walk into my kitchen to get a large glass of water.

"Hey Owen, I'm just making sure you can still make it to the dress appointment." There's no question there and I know this is a reminder call, not a check-in.

I put the call on speaker and scroll through my calendar. "Which dress appointment? Didn't we go looking for dresses last week?"

She lets out a groan. "I still haven't found the dress I'll get married in, bro. That means we need to keep looking."

"Why can't you just take Julie and Emily?" I ask. They are her two very best friends since kindergarten, and it was rough the last time we went wedding dress shopping with them. They didn't like anything I approved of and vice versa.

"Because I want you there. It's just the two of us, O. I know you're having a hard time with your split, but having you there is like having Mom with us."

I can't argue with that. Dad was never in the picture and Mom was incredible, even during the last few days of her life.

"What time?" I ask, pinching the bridge of my nose.

"Ten. I'll send you the address to the boutique. Do you want me to swing by and pick you up?"

"No," I say, a bit forcefully. "I'll be okay. I'm going to have to listen to your friends bicker and joke for the two hours we're there. I don't need to extend that amount by riding in the same vehicle."

"Owen, you're such a grump lately. We need to find you a girl."

I had a girl, I want to say, but she didn't return my feelings.

To be honest, it's been freeing to make my own decisions since the breakup. I was almost a robot with Riley, doing whatever she said. One of the big things she kept me from was hanging out with my friends. I need to get back to doing stuff with the guys because they're the ones still here, checking in and making sure I'm alright. I make a mental note to not let a woman get between me and the guys again. Not that I can see myself in a relationship until I'm forty. Twelve years should be a long enough waiting period before I get serious about anyone again.

"I'll be there by ten. Let me go take a shower."

"So you probably won't make it until ten-thirty," Darcy says, laughing.

I shake my head. "I'll be there. Go get ready." At least I don't have to work for a couple days. I'll have to catch up on sleep after this appointment.

At ten-fifteen, I stroll through the door of the bridal boutique and locate Darcy and her two friends chatting with someone on the couch. I can't quite see the extra person as she's behind one of those headless mannequins donning a wedding dress. Why not put a head on them? It wouldn't be that hard to do and would be way more realistic.

When I'm only a few steps away, all four women turn to look at me and I'm surprised to see Twister-girl from the night before. She's got her foot on the scooter and a note-book in her hand.

"What are you doing here?" she asks, her tone showing her surprise.

"I am here for my baby sister's wedding dress shopping experience. And I take it your job encompasses a lot more than flowers."

Her eyes go wide and pure surprise crosses her face. Sure, I hadn't been the nicest guy last night, but I'm typically a good listener.

"In a sense," she says, glancing back down at her clipboard.

"I'm glad you made it," Darcy says, walking over to give me a quick hug.

I grin at her. "Only a few minutes late. Did I miss the worst part?"

Darcy pokes me in the rib and I jump back, laughing a bit. "Evie is just getting some ideas of what I'm looking for."

We both turn to look at Evie, who nods. "Yep. I think

we've got a good start here. Why don't you come back, Darcy? We'll get started pulling dresses for you to try."

Evie tries to scoot away, but a wheel gets stuck on the rug. She stops and lifts the scooter while balancing on her good leg and then continues down the hall, shaking her head in the process.

Julie and Kim turn to me giggling. "You're back even after the last dress appointment?"

I roll my eyes and wish I could be invisible while still being here. The last dress shopping moment we had, Kim and I practically got in a yelling match because she wants Darcy to wear next to nothing and I'd prefer to have Darcy looking more elegant and mostly covered. It's what Mom would want and I'm trying to channel that energy.

"Well, Darcy says it's important, so I'm trying to be supportive."

Kim gives Julie a quick look and says, "Julie just got out of a relationship. You two should go out sometime."

I paste a smile on my face but inside my flight response is powering on. "I'm not really dating right now. You know, recent breakup and all."

Kim's expression turns into one of bitterness and I settle into a single chair next to the couch, pulling out my phone. Man, I'm just leaving wreckage in my wake. Normal Owen has more tact. I think my filter is officially broken.

There have been a lot of comments over the past couple weeks about my single status and when I'm going to change all that. Maybe I should actually look into the results of the hundred-question test I took to start using the Love, Austen app. Having a computer tell me who I'm best suited to might make things easier than if I keep choosing the wrong woman.

Then I remember that's the last thing I want to do now.

I'm comfortable having no expectations with TheWedding-Planner2 and living my life.

Loyalty is my trump card, and once I'm in a relationship I usually do everything I can to make it work. Hence why I was blindsided by Riley's unexpected betrayal and our subsequent breakup.

I read through my past emails with TheWeddingPlanner2, in part so I don't have to interact with Darcy's friends. Could she actually be a wedding planner or something to do with weddings? Or was it really just a cover for not wanting a relationship, like she said?

I hear a loud thump from around the corner. Maybe it's the nature of my job, but that usually means someone is in trouble.

Tucking my phone into my pocket, I hurry toward the sound and see a mound of white dresses on the floor. Something rustles below it and a head appears after batting away a piece of the white fabric.

"What happened?" I pull back more of the white fabric, trying to figure out what fell over. There is a large silver bar, which was probably holding up at least two dozen dresses moments ago.

Evie blows out a breath, which causes her hair to fly away from her eyes. It's the first time I notice the dark brown with specks of amber. Something about them makes it difficult to look away.

"My scooter got stuck on one of the dresses without me knowing. The bar ended up falling over, taking me with it."

I can't help but smile at this. "Seems like you have bad luck. Did you break a mirror recently?"

The bar isn't heavy and I'm able to pick it up, pulling at least half of the dresses with it. I start lifting the others from the ground to hang back on the rack.

"Break a mirror? Aren't all nurses people of science and don't believe in stuff like that?" Evie asks, pushing up onto her knees.

"We're still people. I just meant that you seem to have gotten into some sticky situations lately."

She stands and rests her splinted foot on the scooter. "Yeah, that's definitely true."

Under her breath, she says, "How am I going to get anything done with this scooter?"

"Can I carry the dresses you need for my sister to the dressing room?" It's against my better judgment, especially because I still get an intense surge of irritation around Evie. But my mother would roll around in her grave if she knew I was being unkind, especially to an injured woman.

Again, she stares at me like I'm growing horns or something and finally says, "Yeah, I don't think I can do it without help."

"Aren't you supposed to be with your client?" a woman with pinched lips asks as she comes from a back room.

Evie takes in a breath and nods. "I'm just pulling dresses now."

"We've got a booked day today. We need to make sure that appointments are no longer than ninety minutes. And I need you to stay late. There are two dresses that need to be finished before their fittings tomorrow."

Evie's shoulders sag even more than they had when I'd offered to help her. "I can probably work that out."

The woman walks out to the showroom floor and I'm surprised that Evie could be so strong toward me and then so quiet and subdued to the woman there.

"Do you like working here, Cinder Evie?" I ask, keeping my tone low.

She turns to look at me, her eyes wide. "I don't know

whether to laugh or be offended by that."

"Well, if it struck a chord, it's probably true."

She doesn't say anything and goes to pick up a dress, looking at it before handing it to me. "There are perks to working here. Mostly the highlight of seeing women glow when they've found the perfect dress."

After another couple minutes, I'm holding four other dresses, not seeing many differences between them. "Are these all the same?"

She shakes her head. "No, there are similar elements. I have to start with a wide range and see what your sister likes."

It's quiet as she wheels back to the dressing room. Once inside, Evie points toward the wall and I hang the dresses, giving my sister a quick smile.

"Thank you for your help," Evie says, making it look like it took everything inside her to say that.

We're off to a great start. Not that we need to have a good start. She's just my sister's wedding dress agent and with the way my sister has turned down dresses, that connection will last only an hour or so. Ninety minutes if her boss has anything to say about it.

She's Kenzie's roommate and good friend, but what Kenzie has said about her doesn't match the person I've met. Motherly and all-knowing were a few of the descriptors. But Evie is just as vulnerable as the rest of us and definitely doesn't look like a mother. Not that I need to be thinking those kinds of thoughts.

Maybe time is the best healer. And maybe it's time for me to be matched. Or just keep life the same.

I like that better. It's best to keep things consistent and avoid the highs and lows that come with a relationship. I'll leave that to the guys.

5

EVIE

Nothing like adding to last night's humiliation by pulling over a rack of dresses on myself. Why did Owen have to be the one to find me?

At least he didn't leave me on the ground. That would've been worse.

I can't focus on him because I have to make up for the time lost. As much as I want to rebel against Judy, she's the shop owner and my boss. I need this job, especially since I'll have the staggering bills from the ER visit coming in. I guess I can always get numbers from Owen right now as a way to make conversation and figure out my budget at the same time.

No, that will definitely cost me my job.

"Okay, Darcy. Let's get you into the first one." I unzip a dress that has small roses sewn into the entire dress. From far away, it's an intricate design, but up close, it's amazing that the stitching could be so consistent.

"What happened to your foot?" Darcy asks. She puts her arms up and I have to shift the scooter forward a little to be able to slip the dress over her head.

Once she's got it situated over her shoulders, I give her a pained smile and say, "I broke it playing Twister."

Darcy's eyebrow raises. "Like the colored dots game?"

"Yep, that's the one."

She gives me a look like she's trying to hide her smile for my sake. "I don't think I've ever heard that happening to someone. Who knew it was such a dangerous game?"

"Right?" I say, trying to come up with another topic to discuss. I know I'll laugh about this later, but Owen sitting out on the couch on the floor is messing with my brain. It's only when I glance in the mirror that I notice how deeply I'm frowning. The guy is going to give me frown lines.

Darcy laughs and says, "I can't decide if you should keep telling people that or make up another story about it."

Nodding, I say, "I've thought about it a few times. Admitting I broke my foot playing a semi-stationary kids' game is very humbling. But I'm not into sports, so I can't tell people I was kicking a football or something."

We get the dress situated and I hold the dress together in back to give her a chance to look at it in the mirror.

"How did your fiancé propose?" I ask, needing to break the silence.

"We've been dating for the past year and he rented a big theater and made a movie for me. It was the cutest thing ever. I turned around to see so many of my friends in the theater with us."

I grin. "That is such a fantastic proposal. Not many women can say their guy made them a movie. He sounds very creative."

Darcy nods and says, "He's in film and movie production. It's always fun to see what he comes up with."

I fluff out the bottom a little, almost losing my balance off the scooter. "What do you think?"

She stares into the mirror and shakes her head. "I don't think this is the one."

"What do you like about this dress?" I ask. That usually helps me pinpoint where to go from here.

"The beading and stitching is really cool, but I don't like the mermaid look. I'm a bit clumsy already and I think if I can't use my full stride, I'd fall on my wedding day. The goal is to avoid that as much as possible."

I smile, and say, "We're two peas in a pod then because clumsy seems to be a thing with me lately."

We get her into a dress she wants to show the group and I let her take the lead, walking out to show her friends and brother. Owen glances up and there's something close to emotion in his gaze. Maybe the Tin Man has a heart after all.

"It's all right," one friend says.

"I don't think it accentuates your body like it should. You need to do a sweetheart neckline," the other friend says.

"I think this one looks good. What do you think, Darcy?" Owen asks.

She turns to look in the mirror again, running her hands down the silky fabric. "I like it, but I don't love it."

"Then let's find something you do love," I say, turning my scooter around so we can head back to the dressing room.

It takes another hour, but Darcy finally says yes to a lovely dress that is flowy and even has pockets. Why would she need pockets the day of her wedding? I'm not sure, but having the option to carry whatever she needs to is a great perk of the dress.

Need lip gloss? Got it.

A tissue to help curb the emotions of the day and save a face of makeup? Check.

How about fresh breath before the first kiss as a married couple? Gum or breath mints to the rescue.

I write pockets onto the mental checklist of things for my some-day wedding dress. My first wedding was at the courthouse, with me in a light blue dress. A girl can hope that there's a second chance out there.

While Darcy is getting changed, I scoot away with her dress over my shoulder to hang it up and then to fill out all the paperwork for it.

"Leave that." Judy's tone is clipped.

"I need to get the client to sign the paper so we can have all the paperwork in order."

"The sleeves on this dress have to be fixed. The bride is hysterical because of it." Judy pushes a dress at me. I glance down at the fabric, cringing because it's not the easiest to tailor. Sometimes I wish I could tell the designers not to use certain fabrics for those of us who have to hem the dress.

"This is the dress the client wants," I say, hanging the dress up next to the computer system. "Will you draw up the paperwork and have them sign it?"

Judy rolls her eyes and says, "In case you forgot, I own this business. I can take care of things just fine."

I bite my lower lip to keep from letting out a retort. I'm not usually combative, but Judy's warnings about time limits and needing to make sales only to have her be so nonchalant about an actual sale is making my head spin.

It takes about fifteen minutes to hem the sleeves. Most of the time is spent fighting the needle and thread with the type of fabric the dress is made of. When I come out with the dress, Darcy and her crew are watching me with confused expressions. "Did Judy get you the paper to sign for your dress?"

Darcy shakes her head. "Not yet. We thought you were putting that together."

Gritting my teeth, I take a deep breath.

I love electricity, food, and paying my bills on time. That's why I put up with this stuff.

It's a thought I've had to use a few times in this job. Making people wait a significant amount of time to sign a simple paper is not how business should be done. But what do I know? I don't own a business.

"Give me two more minutes. I apologize for the delay." I hang up the dress near where Judy is talking with the bride and then walk away. I'm fuming and don't need to jeopardize anything right now.

I get all the paperwork printed and have Darcy sign. She gives me a card to pay for it.

"Is there a payment plan option?" she whispers, glancing over at her friends and brother to make sure they didn't hear.

"Yes," I say, giving her a warm smile. "I'll get that put in now. You'll just need to pay for the deposit and then we'll get the account set up so you'll get a notification monthly to pay for the dress."

"Thank you."

"Thank you for being so patient." I want to talk about how my boss was supposed to help her finalize everything, but I don't want to bash the place that's paying me.

Once the group is on their way out the door, I breathe a sigh of relief that Owen is no longer looming somewhere over my shoulder. I get the impression that he is constantly judging me for everything, and I'm lucky that the dresses falling over was my only mishap of the day.

At least I hope it is.

6

OWEN

Sitting in a bridal boutique is the last place I wanted to be after planning to propose three months ago, but I know how important this is for my sister. We both took it hard when my mother's diagnosis with muscular sclerosis came in, but we had several years to adapt to the differences that came with her condition. The fact it took her life sooner than the doctors predicted was rough. Darcy had many dreams of what her wedding experience should be like, which means I get dragged to shops and asked a million questions about my opinions while trying to say what Mom would do in these situations.

It's funny that the reason I'm a nurse because of my mother's condition. She was a strong, independent woman, raising two kids on her own for most of my life. And she soldiered on through the trials in her health to give us the best life she could. The doctors diagnosed her with MS when I was a preteen and then she lost the battle a year ago when a relapse highlighted a growing mass on her brain, which I wish we'd been able to catch earlier.

As a nurse, I beat myself up thinking about how I

should've been at my mom's side every moment to see the signs, but all I can do now is to be here for my sister.

"The saleswoman is very beautiful," Darcy says, a sly grin forming. Her friends headed out early since they didn't want to wait for the final paperwork to be signed. Who knew there were actually contracts to buy a wedding dress?

Okay, so it's not like buying a car, but I'd only expected to sign the receipt saying that I'd paid for the dress in full. Instead, Darcy made me stand away from the counter while she signed. I caught sight of a payment plan sheet she stuffed into her purse. I'll have to call later and take care of the rest of the cost. Darcy and her soon-to-be husband are both amazing teachers in the Massachusetts school system, but they don't have enough to have a lavish wedding.

Not that I'm rolling in the dough, either. But taking care of my sister is a good use of my money now since I returned the ring and will no longer be planning my own nuptials.

"I didn't notice," I grunt, not sure I want to go down this road at all. Evie is pretty, but there are a lot of similarities to Riley and at the moment, my heart still hurts. The betrayal runs deep.

"You know, I always wondered what Riley's agenda was," Darcy continues.

"She didn't have an agenda. She just decided she didn't love me anymore." I try to focus on something down the road, something in bright yellow.

Darcy turns to look at me. "She never loved you as much as you did her. You practically worshiped the ground she walked on and she took it for granted."

I swallow, not wanting to let the emotions take over now. "Can we please not talk about her? I've been trying to busy myself with anything but this."

"You should take another medical mission trip."

I laugh and shake my head. "A lot of good that did. My life imploded."

"How do you know it wasn't for the better?"

I glimpse myself in the window outside the shop. "Because it was supposed to all fall into place. I've done everything I can to be a dutiful son, brother, and boyfriend. I've even read articles on what to do to be a good future husband."

"Then stop worrying about it. Go have fun. Be the Owen I know you are. Find people to help so you aren't dwelling on your failures."

"I help people in the ER." My defenses are rising and I'm trying to relax a bit. I know she's just trying to help.

"You see them for all of an hour, sometimes up to several hours, and then they're gone. You need a setting where you can connect with people for longer than a day." She pauses a moment. "What about being a hospice nurse or something?"

I've been happy in my career for several years and now she's trying to change it for me.

"I've been volunteering at the senior rehab center and feel pretty good about my time there. I consider that 'helping'."

"I know you're comfortable where you're at, Owen, but you branched out and did something outside your comfort zone by traveling to Guatemala. Maybe it's time you shift to something else. If not that, you can always revenge date."

"What?" I ask, turning to see if she's being serious.

Darcy shrugs. "You know, revenge date. Go on dates with people to spite Riley."

"Wouldn't she have to see me out for that to work?"

"No," Darcy says, putting her hands on my shoulders as if I'm going to flee with the slightest mention of whatever is coming. "It's more of a mental thing for you. Maybe going out with different women will help you figure out if Riley was really the ideal, or if you just held onto the first girl who came your way."

"I'd rather change my career entirely," I say dryly.

"That's not a bad idea. Or change the company you work for."

I narrow my gaze at her. "Why are you so quick to change topics?"

Darcy squirms and turns to look at the traffic down the road. "I feel guilty that I'm getting married and you're struggling after breaking up with Riley."

Shaking my head, I say, "I'm not struggling." I swallow hard, emotion already tightening my throat. "Okay, maybe a little, but you don't need to feel guilty. You and Tom have one of the best relationships I've ever seen."

"You'll find someone, Owen. Someone who makes everything you've been through with Riley seem like the best thing that could've happened to you."

I wish I could agree. Right now my focus is on getting home so I can sleep. Then again, I don't know when I'll be back this way. Maybe I can go in and pay for the rest of the dress now. Get it done before I forget.

"Thanks, sis. I'll see you later."

I wait as Darcy heads toward a parking garage near the shop.

Will I really find someone to share a life with and who won't try to change everything about me?

7

EVIE

"Evelyn, I need you to put this on," Judy says, walking over to me behind the front desk counter. I put away the contract Darcy signed and then started cleaning up anything else that is out of place. It's always better to look busy than to sit around, especially when clients are in the building.

She holds out a dress and practically throws it at me. Checking the tag and the style, this is a designer gown. Sometimes I wonder how Judy got into this business at all with how she treats the clients and the dresses.

"You want me to try on a gown from Sonya James?" I ask, trying to puzzle through her thinking. "I thought we weren't ever supposed—"

"My client can't decide between that dress or the one she has on. You're about the same size. This could be a big sale."

"You don't want to take a picture of each dress for her to see the difference?" I'm already exhausted and it's only lunchtime. My foot is throbbing and the last thing I want to do is squeeze into a wedding dress while trying to balance on one foot.

Judy gives me a familiar glare. "This is the client's request. Hurry and get changed." She turns around and walks back over to the bride and her entourage.

Blowing out a long breath, I toss the dress over my shoulder and make sure it's not dragging anywhere. I have to wrap the train around my neck like a scarf and I'm ready.

Why am I even agreeing to this?

ER bills. Rent. Food.

It takes some maneuvering, but I make it into the dressing room. Several minutes tick by as I change into the dress and hop back over to the scooter. Without even a glance in the mirror, I open the dressing room door.

I can't do up the dress in the back, so I'm trying to hold it together while keeping the bottom away from my scooter wheels. Who knew wheels could be such a danger trap?

It's slow progress, but I finally make it out to the floor.

Judy comes marching toward me with her eyes practically on fire and her jaw set. "What took you so long?" she asks through clenched teeth.

I want to just point to my foot, but I've got to take the high road right now so I do nothing to ruin this very expensive dress. It's worth more than I make in six months.

Judy cinches up the back of the dress, which is almost like a corset with all the long strings. Once she's done, I scooter over next to the platform the bride is standing on. I let the bottom of the dress fall down and try to straighten what I can.

Judy steps closer to the bride. "What do you think about this?"

"Can she lose the scooter? I can't fully picture myself in the dress with it in the way."

"I'm not supposed to put weight—"

"Of course she can," Judy says, sending me a warning look.

From the price of the dress I'm wearing and the one she's got on, I know Judy is seeing dollar signs. She'd be earning money from the smaller ticket dresses too if she put in more effort, but there's only so much I can say.

Instead of sending the scooter wheeling off away from me, I turn it around so the handlebars are behind me. That way my leg is still on the scooter, I have something to balance on, and the dress goes all the way to the floor.

The bride glances between her image and mine in the mirrors. Her entourage is center stage behind us, but I can see them in the reflection whispering about something.

I brush my hands along my backside as discreetly as possible.

That's all I need, to have the back of the dress stuck in my underwear or a hole exposing anything back there. Maybe the handlebars didn't clear the hem of the dress. I turn quickly to see that there's nothing out of place.

"I love that this has the beading up top," the bride says, gesturing to her own dress. "I really love the fuller skirt of that dress, though." She points to the one I'm wearing.

I'm a statue, trying not to move too much so Judy can get the sale. Things have been rough the past couple of months with a newer boutique opening on the other side of the city. But having competition tank a business means this one is not being run how it should.

To be honest, I've thought about putting my application in to work at the other shop, if they have any openings. After the way Judy treated Darcy earlier, along with a host of other things, it's probably time to move on.

"The one you have on is a one of a kind and it wouldn't be difficult to tailor," Judy says, adding in her signature smile. What she's not telling the bride is that it's a one of a kind in every size we have in the back room.

"What about that dress?" The bride is giving me a full-body glance, and while I know she's focused on the dress, I feel self-conscious. I'm usually the best friend or the one helping behind the scenes to make sure everything is just right. Wearing a wedding dress is a mind trip anyway, but to have someone judging me in one is doing things to my brain.

Judy nods and I know what she's thinking. Dollar signs. "That one too."

The dress the bride is wearing is significantly less than the one I have on.

"I think the dress on the help is the one you should go with," one of the bride's friends says with a giggle. "It accentuated your assets very well."

I glance down and remember I have little to accentuate. Then again, the bodice pushes everything up to make it look like I do, at least a cup-size more than normal.

The phone rings at the front desk and I turn to get it, hoping I'll be able to reach the call in time. It's probably the people-pleaser in me, but for weddings, I know how important finding the right dress can be. And even though Judy isn't fazed by the declining business she owns, I'm compelled to do everything I can to save the sinking ship.

"Don't move," the bride commands.

"I'm just going to get this call and I'll be right back." I point toward the ringing phone and scoot forward some more.

"Stay where you are," Judy says. I turn to see her standing in the same spot she was moments before. Why doesn't she try to answer?

One friend stands up and steps in my way.

"Do what she says." Her hands are on her hips.

I suck in a deep breath and say, "Please move. This will give your friend time to think about which dress she wants."

Friend straightens up. I'm a few inches shorter even with the small boost the scooter gives me, but at this point, I've barely survived a broken foot so far. Could I really survive assault?

"This is one of the biggest decisions of Tracy's life and you're not going to move until she's decided which dress is hers."

I veer my scooter to the side and push past her. The phone is still ringing and the bell above the door rings, turning my attention to whoever is walking in.

"Welcome to Bridal Oa–" I start to say and stop when I see Owen. With the distraction, I must've dropped the bottom of the dress and rolled over the hem of the dress I'm wearing. The force of it pitches me forward and I'm on the ground, staring up at the plain white ceiling.

I'm going to need directions to the next available cave. Hibernation sounds ideal right now.

The group laughs and I'm wishing I were at home, curled up watching some of my favorite comfort movies.

I close my eyes for a brief second to ready myself for the humiliation I'll receive.

When I open my eyes, I see Owen, of all people, kneeling next to me. "Are you all right?" he asks.

Why do I feel like this is a Sleeping Beauty situation? Nope, not going to happen.

I nod. "I'm good. Just running a clumsy streak."

"She's going to be fine," says one of the bride's friends. They're probably silently chuckling at this point.

He stares into my eyes and then grabs my wrist with his thumb and pointer finger. I freeze, not sure what he's doing.

The guy lets go of my wrist and I sit up, trying to figure out if I'm part of some strange dream or if I made it all up during the fall.

"I don't know," he says, looking up at the woman who had stood in my path. "From my angle, it looked like you hit her." Turning to me, he asks, "Did she hit you?"

What? I basically threw myself on the ground because of my stubbornness. "Um," I say, trying to figure out what he's planning. He's been all grumpy ever since I met him and besides the sweet moments between him and his sister, I know nothing else about him. Is he a jokester? Not sure. Would he lie about something like this just to attack people he doesn't know?

"There's no way. I only stood in the way to help Tracy make a decision. Please, she just needs to decide which dress to buy." And now the woman who had acted like the bodyguard dissolves into tears. "I'm so tired. She just needs to pick a dress."

I glance over at Owen and then back at the woman. The bride is wide-eyed with her mouth open, as if she's just witnessed a crime.

Owen reaches out his hand toward me and I hesitate before realizing this is déjà vu from what happened an hour ago in the back room. Again, contact with his skin sends a ripple of something traveling the length of my arm. He deposits me next to my scooter and says, "No walking on your boot."

I can't tell if he's joking or taking his job as a nurse extra seriously. All I can do is nod.

I trudge back to the platform since the call stopped ringing what seems like an hour ago, not excited about the idea of being a Barbie doll. Then it's like my brain comes into focus again and I turn back to Owen.

"Did we forget something?" I ask, trying to block out the fact that I'm wearing a wedding dress.

Owen startles, like he was in another world and says, "I think I left my wallet in here." He turns to where he'd been seated and walks over to pick something up from under the chair. He waves a small brown bifold and says, "Found it."

I don't think there was actually anything on the ground. What's he playing at?

This has to be the most cordial he's been since our meeting in the ER last night.

"I think I want the dress she's wearing. I'd like to try it on again." The bride's whine grates on my nerves, but I breathe out a sigh of relief and hurry toward the dressing room.

"Awesome, I'll go change." Get me out of this dress and this situation.

I've already made it to the dressing room, but I have to slow down for Judy to join me. In the interim, I hear the bride's high-pitched and now emotional voice asking why her friend is mad at her. It would be stress relieving to tell the bride that her friends are sick of the indecisions and shop-hopping. Nothing like reliving the petty high school fights while trying on dresses.

Judy appears, saying nothing as she unties the strings on the back of my dress.

"I'll get changed and head in to tailor one of the dresses," I say, hating the silence in the room. What I hate more is that I can't say what I really want to.

"See that you do."

A response comes to the surface, but I shake my head and walk out of sight. I don't need much, but I do want respect for things that I have tried to do. Even though I have a job, I still feel aimless, like I haven't quite figured out what I want to do for my future.

Fully dressed, I scoot through the main floor to the other wing where all the tailoring supplies are. But just as I make it to the door, I see movement by the front counter.

Owen.

Letting out a deep sigh, I turn the scooter to the counter and say, "Is there something I can help you with?"

He nods. "I think Darcy made a payment plan for her dress. I just want to pay off the rest of it now, if possible."

His words surprise me to where my mouth no longer works. Either that or the connection between it and my brain has been severed.

Grumpy Owen is actually kind of sweet to his sister.

He holds out a credit card and raises an eyebrow, like I've lost my mind. Which is probably spot on at this point.

"Give me a moment," I say, tapping on the keyboard. I log back in and pull up Darcy's account. "You want to pay the remaining balance of $1824.36?"

Owen nods, holding out his card once again. I take it from him and get shocked in the meantime.

"Sorry," I mutter, trying to focus on the task at hand and not the fact that I'm an electrically charged being from all the scootering I've done lately.

I input his card and charge it. When the receipt is printing out, Owen waves it off. "I don't need the receipt. Thanks."

He turns toward the door and I take the paper and place it inside the folder in the desk drawer. I also take a screenshot of the paid invoice and put it in the digital folder on the computer screen.

"What did you do?" Judy says, looking a lot like the cartoon of Cruella DeVil as she comes at me, her eyes wide and her hair flying in several directions.

"I just charged his card," I say, trying to come up with a scenario that might've contributed to her rage.

Judy holds up a wedding dress and I realize it's the one I was just wearing. "You've ruined it. The beads broke here." She holds it up so close to my face that I can't even focus on the spot she's talking about.

"I can fix it." That's all I can think of to say. I've had to fix worse things since I started working here and a few extra beads won't be hard.

"The bride won't want it now," Judy says. My gaze turns to the entourage, but the bride is gone. She must've gone into the changing room to get ready for the new dress.

"Did you ask her?" I say, trying to keep calm. "I've fixed a ton of dresses. There are only a handful of beads I'd have to fix."

"We won't say anything," the friend who was in tears says. It's like she'll do anything to get out of this store.

Judy shakes her head. "This will have to come out of your paycheck."

"That's fine. I'd say it's about $100, right?"

"No, the entire dress."

And I've become a puppet, limp and trying to find my voice. "You can't be serious."

"There's no way I can sell this now. You'll have to work it off."

"That's a twenty-thousand-dollar dress that can be fixed and still sold at full-price."

There is a long pause and Judy says, "It won't now—"

"You are the one who made me try it on!" I say, my patience wearing thin.

"You ruined it by running to answer the phone when we were trying to make a sale. You should've let the phone go to voicemail."

And that's when I have no restraint left. "Forgive me for trying to help your company earn business."

Judy looks as though I've just slapped her. It's only then I register all the eyes on us. At least Owen left already. I've suffered enough embarrassment with him present.

"You'll start paying this week," Judy says.

My brain goes through the evidence here. I doubt her claims would be backed up, especially since the dress is pretty much perfect. And even though I hate getting into trouble or causing waves, there's no way I can lock myself into this for years to come.

"I quit."

Judy blinks a few times and says, "What?"

"I quit. I won't be responsible for a dress you both asked me to put on and won't let me take the time to fix."

And before I lose my nerve, I wheel myself into the back room and grab my purse and any belongings there. Coming back in is not an option.

The room is dead quiet with everyone staring at me as I wheel toward the front door.

"You can't just leave like that," Judy says, her voice strangled.

"I've tried to help you, Judy. I've stayed late without pay and done everything I could to help your business succeed. If you'd care about some of the budget dresses the way you do about this bride, this place would be booming. Yesterday was exceptional with the number of women who came in for appointments, but having only two clients scheduled for a ten-hour day is not a good sign. I thought I had won the jackpot when I was hired here. You had a reputation that I thought would help me in this industry, to learn all the ins and outs. I can't justify spending anymore of my sanity here, especially when you want to saddle me with a dress I didn't ruin. Thanks, but no thanks."

I get to the door and wish I could walk normally because the struggling to get the door open and the scooter down the step to reach the sidewalk takes away some of the drama of an impressive exit. I've never been one for the stage, but I can see the appeal.

I finally make it out the door when I see Owen leaning up against the building. When did he come out here?

"That was quite the show," he says, giving me a ghost of a smile.

My stomach drops. "You saw it?"

"I was barely out the door when I heard yelling. I turned around to make sure you hadn't fallen or something again."

Awesome. I'll always be remembered in his mind as the woman who's falling whenever he's around. Not that he's the cause, of course.

"Too bad I didn't prepare for it. I could've set up cameras and gotten the footage. My brother would never believe I would do something like that." My middle brother, Drew, had explained quitting from the advertising company he worked for a couple of years ago was both liberating and terrifying. I can now understand what he means.

"I'm sure people would've popped some popcorn just to watch the entertainment."

"Probably." Everything that just happened has made me tired all of a sudden, not to mention that I didn't get the best night's sleep ever. I pull out my phone to get an Uber. This will be the last one I can splurge on for a while, at least until I figure out what to do with my life.

"Do you need help to get home?" Owen asks, glancing down at the scooter and my foot.

Shaking my head, I hold up my phone with the car

reservation. "No, it looks like Leo should be here in about five minutes."

Something about his hesitation makes me curious about him. He's been so grumpy ever since we met, all of twelve hours ago. I should give him the benefit of the doubt.

He nods and waves as he walks toward the T station. The man is so mysterious, I'm not sure where to start when analyzing our interactions together. But maybe I should put that off completely. I've just lost my job and the way to provide for myself. That's my first priority now.

8

OWEN

Jack: We missed you this morning. Movie?

I check the text and try to figure out the day. I'm running on three hours of sleep from nearly twenty hours ago and it's getting harder to function.

Owen: Rain check? I just finished wedding dress shopping, and I have to get to Rosewood Senior Center.

Jack: Wait, what are you talking about? Are you getting married to someone you met in the past twelve hours?

I laugh, shaking my head. The only new people I have met in that time were Evie and the other roommate with the red hair. And while Evie's departure from her job was priceless, I'm not ready for Mrs. Young yet.

With a few words, I tell him about Darcy's wedding and how she wanted my opinion on the dress.

Owen: What do you know about Evie Evans?

Right after typing that, I know I've made a mistake. Jack has never been one for letting something go. He's like a hound going hunting.

Jack: What are you hoping to find out? ;)

Why am I curious? Because I've been around her twice,

three times if I count my leaving the bridal shop and going back in, and each time there has been some unpredictability there. Mostly trips and falls, but it's such a switch to watch her pop up as if nothing happened and keep going about life. If I'd fallen as much as she has, I would probably hide out at home until I was sure the bad luck had passed.

Instead of answering Jack, I tuck my phone back into my jacket and rest my head against the glass of the T train. The past weeks have differed from anything before. From my trip to Guatemala and breaking up with Riley, to volunteering at Rosewood and meeting Gordon Attenbury, one of the residents, it's like I've been on one of those rides that jerks from one way to the other so unexpectedly that you can't really gain your bearings. Then again, the last couple weeks have been better and I can feel myself finally breathing normally.

For the hundredth time, I go over what happened in my past relationship. But now Darcy's words echo back to me. I can see how I might've been over the top with the romance, but did Riley never really love me? We'd talked about the future a bunch, about what our lives would look like together. I'd always thought she was into it, but now I'm wondering if I was just hoping she'd jump into my little car like in the game of LIFE and that we'd make the most of our life through the ups and downs. I guess I'm not even winning in a fictional story, either.

I open my eyes to see we're coming up on my stop, and I'm excited to be just a few minutes away from a good sleep.

Four hours. I can get that much in before I should stop by Rosewood at dinner time. I started working there as a volunteer before leaving for Guatemala. Mike, one guy I went to nursing school with, moved back here after a quick stint in Indiana and manages the schedule for the center. He roped me into volunteering and it's one of the best things I could've done, for my own mental health anyway.

Gordon and I have a weekly game of trivia watching Jeopardy and trying to outguess each other. I'm pretty sure he's winning by at least a hundred at this point.

The guy smiles about everything, even when we have to scrape off dead tissue around a large wound in his leg.

We've formed an unlikely friendship after I had to fill in for one of the other nurses on their rounds one day. He's told me about life with his wife, Vera, and all the heartbreaks it took to get to her. I wish I could say the stories make me optimistic about my future love life, but I'm not at that point yet.

Maybe I'll go now. I'm exhausted, but I've got a free weekend ahead of me. I'd rather sleep with no obligations on my schedule than have to wake up before visiting hours are over. It won't be Jeopardy time, but I'll tell him I'll make up for it twice next week.

"Gordon," I say, walking into his room with a wide smile twenty minutes later. I glance out the door to see if anyone is walking by and pull out a small box of chocolates I bought on the way here. "Look what I snuck in."

His eyes go wide and he grins. "I'll have to put in my dentures to eat those," he says.

"I know you said they're your favorite. But you have to promise me you'll only eat one a day so your sugars don't skyrocket." I take a seat on the chair next to him for a minute.

"I think I can do that. Did you hear? They're releasing me tomorrow."

Part of me is sad to have him gone. He's been a sort of father figure to me the past few weeks. Not that I know what a father is like in my life, but this was closer than anything before.

"That's great, Gordon. I'll miss our trivia nights."

He nods. "I'm ready to be home. I've been in this place, which is nice, don't get me wrong," he says, holding out his hand as if to emphasize his words, "but there's something about being home that helps a person heal. And we don't have to give those up. I'll write my address so you can still come over."

I turn over his words in my mind. "That would be great. I look forward to beating you at *Jeopardy* one day." I laugh and then think about his last words. "My mom was in a facility like this for a while. She'd broken her hip after a nasty fall and she wasn't making very much progress. I asked if we could take her home and I'd help her while I was on break from nursing school. You would've thought she had taken some magic pills or something after the improvement she made so quickly."

Gordon gives me a strange look and says, "That's interesting coming from a man who's working here."

"I'm a volunteer," I say. "Now that you'll be a jailbird, breaking free of here, what do you recommend they change or fix? Mike is hoping to get some input to revamp a few areas. Is there anything that you wished we had or could do while here?"

Tapping his lips with his finger, Gordon says, "I'll have to think about that. I mean, I had plenty of company with you visiting. It would be lonely without someone to check up on me."

"What's it like when you go home?" I ask. He'd talked about how he and Vera couldn't have kids, and his relatives were mostly dead or had moved to other states.

Instead of getting a sad look on his face, he's got the

widest grin I've ever seen from him. "Well, I'll have you when you can make it and I've got my next-door neighbors to cheer me up."

We've talked a lot about life, but I'm trying to picture neighbors about the age he is making him laugh.

"Do you live in an older neighborhood?" I ask, trying to picture it.

He shakes his head. "Nope, next door are several young women who are all roommates. We're in a prank war."

I stare at his face, waiting to laugh at his joke. "You're in a prank war? How have we not talked about this before?"

"Yeah. Don't look so shocked. And I just remembered about the pranks. I've been in here a few weeks, you know. A lot has been going on. But this guy has skills for being in his eighties." He points to himself and then winks.

Laughing, I say, "Your moves are probably what started your road to a rehab facility."

He glares at me a few seconds before saying, "I probably deserved that. I've only waved to them, but they seem like nice girls. The pranks get me out of bed every day. You could always date one of them. I don't see many men stopping by." He pauses a moment, unwrapping one of the chocolates I brought. "How is your pen pal, by the way?"

Gordon is the only one I've told about TheWedding-Planner2. It's all just casual anyway, but I like that he doesn't try to make something out of nothing. A guy and a woman can be friends. It doesn't always have to be about ending up together.

"Good. We've been talking about our favorite foods. She's well-traveled, and I've got a running list of things I need to try in different countries when I go."

"Are you heading on a long trip soon?" Gordon asks.

I shake my head. "I wish. Once I'm established here and

help my sister get through her wedding. Without our mom here, she's having a hard time."

Gordon nods. "Yes, that's when a woman has the hardest time, I think. Vera's father didn't approve of our marriage, which was difficult. And in those times, it was hard for a wife to go against her husband, even to attend the wedding of her only daughter. Her mother wrote her a letter that Vera kept throughout the years and cherished throughout our marriage. I remember a lot of crying moments because of that. But Vera told me every day that she never regretted marrying me. The wedding is one day, but a marriage is a lifetime."

This guy is full of great one-liners. I should probably buy a notebook and carry it around when I chat with him. I think back to Riley and what a wedding with her would've looked like. She'd have invited all of Boston if she could and rented the fanciest spot in the city to get married. I'd be okay with a lake house or a courtroom, as long as the people who mattered most were there.

But those only bring up bitter memories at the moment.

"Tell me more about these pranks," I ask. "How did it get started?"

With a smile, Gordon leans his head back against the bed and says, "It was in the spring. I'd just gotten home from here after healing a broken hip. Troy was my home health nurse and came in madder than a hornet one day because some teens had toilet papered my trees outside. I told him that it's a lot better they're out doing that than things that could get them arrested. The neighbor heard me say something and we've formed a bond over pranking each other every so often. Those are some of the happiest times these past two years."

I see the sadness there. He's thinking about Vera again,

and I wonder if I'll ever find someone to feel that deeply about.

"That sounds like fun. But how are you going to keep up the war with your leg like this? You won't be able to go walking around the yard for more than a couple of minutes." The wound in his shin looks much better than it did a couple of weeks ago, but I can tell it's still painful at times. He'll have to have another home health nurse come check on it, but he's passed off everything to return home.

Gordon says, "Why don't you come help me?"

"You want me to take part in your prank war?" I say, laughing.

"Yeah, why not? It would give you something to do, and I can always use the company." He gets teary-eyed.

Nodding, I say, "Okay, I'll do it. Just not tomorrow. I need a good long sleep and a breathtaking hike." I don't know if it's because of the emotions coursing through him or the fact that I don't want to think of him being so lonely that I agree.

There's a knock on the door behind me and I stand, giving him a nod. "I'll get you my information before you head out."

Owen Young taking part in a prank war. That's not something I've ever been a part of.

Maybe it will be just the thing to take my mind off my strange life.

9

EVIE

I just quit my job. That's going to take a while to sink in. Taking an Uber home is the best decision I've ever made. Well, in the last twenty-four hours, anyway. The problem is that they're expensive now that I'm no longer earning money.

My face goes hot as I think about my last encounter with Judy. While it was an adrenaline rush to see her reaction when I announced I was done, I'm now panicking that I won't have money coming in for a bit. After everything that had gone wrong this morning, my mind is dancing at three times the normal speed. Think about listening to audiobooks at three times the speed. I've only made it to 2x, or a little faster, depending on the narrator.

I just quit my job. I've never done that without careful planning and securing another job beforehand.

With a few clicks, I log into my bank account on my phone to check the balance. After a few calculations, I know I'll be okay for at least six months. I just don't want to go running to Dad for money.

My parents set up a trust for each of their children when

we were born. We used the money for college and then have a monthly stipend type-thing after. And I'm super grateful for that. It made it easier to study and take part in all the extracurricular groups while in school without having to worry about the basic necessities.

Then my older brother Luke went and ruined the process by not getting married on my father's timeline, and my other brother Drew quit his job in advertising and began managing the apartment buildings he owns. We were all turning out to be a disappointment to our father and he's made certain stipulations to opening the trust again. Mine is that I have to be married.

I refuse to marry someone just to get my trust fund back. And while there has been a significant learning curve to managing money over the past two years, I think I've got the hang of it. Mostly.

Without a paycheck from last week and now not getting one because of quitting, things are about to get interesting. At least I stocked up on some extra meat and food with my last paycheck. I'll have to get creative with how I stretch it all to last.

The cab pulls up in front of our house and I look around, wondering if my last prank has been reciprocated yet.

It's been almost a week since the last prank. From my eighty-year-old neighbor.

That sounds more like a confessional than the good-natured fun it actually is. Anytime I see him outside after decorating his yard in lawn gnomes or sprinkling bird seed all over, I'm just as happy as he is about our prank war.

Did I grow up pulling pranks on people? No.

I'd heard about the hazing of teams and groups in high school and college, but never had to worry about those. But when I heard my neighbor praise a bunch of teenagers for toilet papering his yard, I figured I could continue this. I'm several years out of being a teenager, but planning and executing the pranks has been beneficial for my own mental health. It gives me a purpose and feels like a service to my elderly neighbor.

The neighbor is just as into the pranks as I am, which makes it all worth it. At this point, I should probably get to know his name and a bit more about him.

The first prank I did was get all the discounted Easter decor from the store (#budgetproblems) and set it up all over his front yard, complete with filled eggs. I'd given him a hint about me being the decorator next door and within two days, he covered our front yard in newspapers. It had already rained, meaning it was clumpy when we went to pick it up.

We've been trading off with the pranks for the past five months, and I've usually been at work when the pranks have been cleaned up in his yard and a new one done to ours. I haven't seen anyone else living at his house, but maybe it's a healthcare worker who helps him with it?

My favorite, by far, were the giant blow-up pool animals they put all over the yard. Those showed up about the time Trey and Kenzie started hanging out. Now they're dating and all lovey-dovey, which is sometimes cute and sometimes gag-worthy.

I haven't seen the home health vehicle in my neighbor's driveway in a few days and I worry something happened. Maybe they had to take him to a facility? I've meant to actually meet him, but life just gets in the way.

I might have to scoot my way next door and see.

But for now, I need some comfy clothes and a pan of cinnamon rolls after the day I've had. I just don't have the energy to make them. And using up a few sticks of butter on one dessert might not be the wisest choice. Tightening belt strings and all that. Or is it supposed to be purse strings?

"Hey, what's up?" Millie asks, glancing up from her phone where she's seated at the kitchen table. It's unusual to see her at the house during the day, since she's usually corralling kids. The ones who contributed to the pain in my foot.

"Oh you know, I quit my job today."

Millie's eyes go wide and she says, "Me too. Well, actually, I quit yesterday."

That gives me a jolt of energy. "Really? What happened? You didn't say anything at the hospital last night."

Millie is from a small town in Wyoming and she's the sweetest person I know. I didn't think she had it in her to quit.

"I asked for a few days off because Beau was coming into town and they refused to let me off even a little early. When I asked a month ago, my boss acted like that wouldn't be a big deal." Millie slumps over the table. "I haven't had a full day off in over a month, Evie. The closest I got was our mud run, but I still had to go back and help with the kids after that. And when I said I had to go be with you at the hospital, they flipped. To not have the freedom to go help a friend in need is not how I want to live my life. I'm a nanny, not their actual parent, but the lines were almost non-existent there. Kenzie picked me up from their house on the way to the hospital. So now I'm trying to figure out what to do."

"Amen, sister," I say. "Now we need to get out of the unemployment lane." I sit down on one of the chairs. My knee is thanking me for the reprieve of not supporting my whole body on the scooter for a few minutes.

"What happened? Was it because of your foot?"

I shrug, trying to go over the events of the day with a more outside perspective. "I mean, hobbling around and trying to guide a scooter while carrying long wedding dresses didn't help the situation. A brother of one of the clients helped me carry some of them."

Millie leans in with a conspiratorial gleam in her eyes. "Was he cute?"

"He was actually the nurse from the ER last night. Owen?"

She blinks a few moments as I wait for her response. "What are the odds?"

Shaking my head, I say, "Not high, that's for sure. I mean, he was crusty in the ER, and he softened just a bit, but the man has a serious vendetta against all things bride and groom."

"He probably just went through a breakup."

I grin. "You look like you've just gone through one yourself."

Millie takes a deep breath and nods. "It feels like it. I mean, I've been so close to the kids for months now and it's like they just got ripped away from me. Which makes no sense because I'm the one who quit."

"Do you have any plans to find another job? Or do you want to keep nannying?"

"I don't know what else I would do. I mean, I have skills, but most of them involve entertaining people a fraction of my age or wilderness survival."

"You could always ask your brother if he has something for you. Isn't he starting up a company with Spencer?"

Millie nods. "Yeah, they're going to do some kind of production thing. It's funny that Beau talked about Spencer so much, and it's the same one we've been hanging out with for the last few months. Small, small world, even in the big city of Boston."

"Really? How did they meet?"

"Beau went to college out here. He's actually the one who convinced me to get a job in Boston. I love where I'm from, but I needed a change. When you live in a town with only a few thousand people, it gets old knowing just about everyone and their dirty laundry."

I shake my head, trying to picture it. "That would be hard. Don't give up. I'm definitely not going to."

The words feel empty as they go through me. A gal can only change jobs so often and so completely before she runs out of options. Unlike Kenzie, who's managed to establish herself as an organizational genius, my skills are getting smaller and smaller when it comes to available jobs.

I think about the jewelry I made that's still sitting in my bedroom. As much as I love creating unique pieces, I'm not sure I could make a living out of selling them.

The thing I get the most excited about is helping women feel confident and excited to find a dress, no matter the size, style, or requirements. It's like a mystery as I go through several of the options.

What can I do with that now that I don't work for Judy anymore?

Apply at the new boutique.

I think about Darcy. Her mother is gone, and I know how hard that is when getting married. If she had her mother's wedding dress, I could repurpose it. I've seen so many fun transitions of using pieces of a sentimental dress to add to a newer wedding dress or even make a robe to wear while getting hair and makeup done the day of.

My brain is spinning as I think of the possibilities. It makes me think of those little special bears people have made with the shirts or clothing of the special person who's passed on. A lump comes to my throat as I think about that. I could start by taking some of my mother's clothes and making a stuffed bear for my niece.

It's been a while since I've been this excited about anything. I'm not sure where to start other than with some of my own stuff to showcase my talent, but that's something to keep me going. And it would touch hearts, which is something I absolutely thrive on.

"Who's turn is it to cook?" I ask. I stand and scoot over to the fridge, not sure what we have, but my stomach growls in response. It's still a little early for dinner, but I might as well get something going.

"Hillary's."

I nod, knowing that chances of her cooking are slim. The woman is amazing, but staying focused on any household task is difficult.

Our system of taking turns making dinner worked well when there were more of us at the house consistently. Kenzie still lives here despite being engaged to Trey, but her cooking skills extend to burning mac and cheese. Hillary would rather just order takeout every meal and while it's nice in a pinch, there's something amazing about a home-cooked meal.

I take out cheese, tomatoes, and bread. Pulling the butter dish from the cupboard and then a pan from the clean dishes pile, I set to making a grilled cheese and tomato sandwich.

"Where did you learn how to cook?" Millie asks, walking over and leaning against the counter. She's watching my movements as if taking mental notes. Even though we've been roommates for several months, I can count the number of times Millie has been home for dinner on one hand because of her work schedule as a nanny.

"That's a great question. I actually grew up in a house with a full-time cook."

"Really? That sounds like heaven."

"Fran could make some amazing meals out of the least ingredients. I used to go sit in the kitchen and watch her when I had nothing to do. Being the youngest and the only girl meant I had a lot of freedom. I wasn't going to be taking over the family business, so I could roam where I wanted."

Millie smiles and nods. "I learned whatever I could while reading a recipe. But then I would pretend to mess it up so I wasn't in charge of cooking every meal made at home."

The front door opens and a few seconds later, Kenzie strolls in. She looks like she's been through a sandstorm in the Sahara Desert. Dust covers every inch of her clothes and face.

"What happened?" Millie and I say at the same time.

"My shop vac blew. I'd just spent an hour cleaning out this guy's garage and it looks like nothing changed from when I first got there. So I'll have to go back tomorrow."

I motion to the skillet and say, "Are you up for a tomato and cheese sandwich?"

She gives me a pained look. "There's no bacon or meat in there?"

Laughing, I say, "I'm just working with what we've got."

"Yeah, I'll try it out. I'm going to go shower before our house looks like an antique shop from all this dust."

I place a lid over the pan, allowing the cheese to melt a bit more than normal and slow down the browning of the bread. Millie must've disappeared upstairs, leaving me alone. I pull out my phone and check my messages from HuskyHiker521.

It's almost an unconscious response now. Check email. Check Love, Austen messages.

We never did a pen pal program in school, and I always loved the stories of people who met up with their pen pal years later. It doesn't help that those usually lead to romance.

Not that I have high hopes of that with HuskyHiker. To be honest, it's just nice to get insights into a male brain without jumping through hoops and needing some kind of crystal ball to interpret. I've never been able to talk to men with the ease that Hillary does, the conversations usually go through some awkward spots because I struggle to have attention on me for too long.

There's only a brief message this time.

I got your message. It's been a long day, but I didn't want you to think I forgot. Expect a message tomorrow.

As much as I would've loved the answers to my random questions from my last message, I smile at the thoughtfulness of the guy. I hadn't even told him my scary tales of being ghosted by men before to have this response.

I grin and tap out a longer response with more questions. Hopefully, he'll answer them. Because I'm all sorts of confused about the grumpy nurse and maybe my pen pal will have answers of whether his actions were normal. I just have to keep it generalized. Like Millie says, Boston is turning into a smaller world every day, and it would be awkward if my pen pal knows Owen.

But then again, when have I worried about life being awkward? I'm sure Owen thinks I'm the biggest klutz on this side of the Charles River.

10

OWEN

I did it. I took my sister's advice and I'm on a revenge date with Denise, a nurse that I've worked with before.

She'd texted me asking if I could switch her shifts next week and I said yes before asking her out on a date. I'm not sure how she took it when she got the text, but she's been all smiles and chatter since I picked her up.

"I'm surprised you asked me out," Denise says. "Did you and Riley break up?"

Something about her words and her facial expression isn't jiving. Does she already know about the implosion of my relationship with my ex and she just wants the juicy details? Or is she really oblivious?

I nod. "Yeah, almost three months ago."

She bats her eyelashes at me. "Am I your first date since then?"

How do I respond to that? It's been five minutes into this revenge date and I'm thinking this is a huge mistake. Sure, Denise could go into work tomorrow and tell all her coworkers she went on a date with me, which was the primary reason I chose her. The girl can talk.

The drawback is she didn't know Riley and I had broken up. The more I study her face, I'm convinced she definitely knew.

But what is the benefit of having her blab it to everyone? To make Riley jealous?

A normal person would say, "Duh, that's why it's called revenge."

I'm beginning to see that our relationship was more one-sided than I thought. Riley gave up almost nothing, whereas I had to skip out on friend-time around ninety percent of the time and completely change my eating habits. I mean, I ate wheatgrass smoothies daily when with her. They are probably the worst thing ever invented by humans. Not that I don't enjoy eating healthy-ish, but a pizza now and then won't kill me.

When it's time, I want a love story like Gordon and Vera. Well, not the ostracizing from parents, but that they loved each other so much that they made it through the obstacles.

"No," I say, answering her question. Technically yes, but I'll pretend dress shopping with my sister counts as a date. Evie was there and she's a lot more normal, albeit clumsy, than the woman in front of me.

We're sitting at a small restaurant that serves shrimp, crab and other fish by the bag. I've been thinking about the food here for days and figured it would serve a two-for-one purpose.

Denise looks at the menu. "Is this all they have? Fish stuff?"

I cringe. Please tell me she's not allergic.

"I think so. I've never been here before. Do you have allergies?" Don't say it.

"No, I'm just not a fan of the taste."

Nodding, I say, "You don't want to try it once?"

She looks between me and the menu, as if weighing her options. Letting out a deep sigh, she says, "Okay, I'll try it out. But if it's disgusting, there will be no goodnight kiss."

I choke on pure air. A kiss is not on the menu for our date.

I'm going to kill Darcy. Has she revenge dated? I'll have to ask her more about it when I get home. Because if she's giving untried opinions, we're going to have words.

We chat here and there about little things and about working at the hospital, but I've pretty much run out of things to say. I didn't think that was possible, because my messages with TheWeddingPlanner2 are always a continuation of our past conversations, weaving into an endless conversation.

Then again, Denise is doing all the talking for the both of us.

"My friend is getting engaged soon. Her fiancé is so good-looking and nice. I mean, he came over with her to help me pack when I was moving apartments. They stayed the whole time, which is more than what my brothers did."

All I can do is nod and glance over at the kitchen every five seconds, hoping the food will come out.

When it finally does, I nearly sigh out loud. Now I can have peace while I eat.

"Ew," Denise says, holding up a piece of shrimp between her thumb and forefinger.

"Just take a bite. Try it. If you don't like it, you can order something else." There's no way I could finish two bags of shellfish, but I can always take it home if she doesn't eat it. Win, win.

She takes a bite and says, "Okay, it's not terrible. But my hands are so slimy with the butter and everything."

I'm going to get a commentary every minute of this. I focus on my food, cracking the crab legs and working to get all the little pieces of meat out of there with the itty-bitty fork.

Forty-five minutes later, we finish the meal and I drive her home. As tempted as I am to open the door and wave goodbye, I was raised better. So I stand several inches away from her and don't climb the steps to her door before I say goodnight.

It's such a relief to drop her off that the silence in the car is like a lullaby for me and it's hard to stay awake.

Revenge dating is not for me.

11

EVIE

I glance out at our yard Saturday morning, still all neat and clean. It looks so strange since we've had some prank or another happening for the past few months. It usually takes a few days for me to clean up anything that my neighbor has come up with, and I didn't realize how much I've missed the excitement of the surprise.

He's got to be in a facility for his health, and I just hope he's doing okay. I should've gone over a lot sooner to fully introduce myself, but life has a way of taking away the time. Then again, being jobless makes it seem like I have all the time in the world.

I check my messages for anything from HuskyHiker521 and then scroll on the internet to get an idea of another prank. It's getting harder to find fun and friendly pranks because most of them are the ones you do to sworn enemies and hope to never get caught. We don't do that here. I'm going to have to get creative so it can stay all in good fun.

My favorite prank that I've done was spreading out Pop Rocks and waiting for the sprinklers to come on. It sounded like firework poppers for at least an hour while the water was on. The grass didn't suffer from it either, so that's a good thing.

I scroll down and see an idea that says, "Signs in the yard."

Perfect, that's an inexpensive one. All I need is a bunch of poster boards. And to get out of the house to go get it. Thank you bum leg for making normal things that much harder.

My phone rings and it's Millie. "Hey girl," I say, sitting back on the large couch we have upstairs. It's the best spot to have my foot elevated in the house.

"Hey, I'm at the store. Do we have minced garlic? I thought we did, but didn't want to leave without checking."

I remember throwing the bottle away the last time I cooked. "We are all out. Hey, while you're there, will you pick up like ten sheets of poster paper? Different colors will work as long as it's not black."

"Are you planning to run for student council?" Millie asks, chuckling. It makes me laugh that she's laughing.

"Not quite. It's for my next prank."

"Of course. Okay, I'll grab that and be home soon. I'll see if it fits in my little cart."

It's only then that I remember she doesn't have the car she used to drive around from her employers. "Wait, how did you get there?"

"I took the bus after my interview."

I sigh. "Don't worry about it then. I'll find some later." I don't want her to have to struggle to get poster board home while also wrangling groceries.

An hour later, Millie shows up with five bags of groceries, a gallon of milk, and the requested paper. "I told you not to worry about it," I say.

"I know, but this is something to take your mind off

being jobless. And I figured I could help you with whatever it is you're planning. The panic of not having a job and all the expenses adding up is getting to me."

We grab all the permanent markers in the house and start working on the various signs we'll hang up.

It takes at least three hours and I'm surprised how artistic Millie is. She uses different fonts on the different sayings.

"How are we going to get these to stand up?" Millie asks, snapping the lid onto a marker after she finished her last board.

I frown. I hadn't thought of that part. "Do we have any wood sticks out back?"

The sad part is I already know the answer. There's no fireplace or wood stove in our house, so it's not like we've got a stack of wood waiting to be burned out back. I don't have wire or anything like that either.

"What if we use rope or twine and just tape the posters to it?" Millie says.

"That could work. Do you know if we have any?"

She nods. "I took everything I purchased for the kids' art stuff and anything else I bought with my own money for the kids before I left." Her smile turns to sadness and I'm sure she's thinking about the kids she nannied for.

Millie leaves the room and, a few minutes later, comes back with an enormous ball of a thick twine and a roll of duct tape. "I didn't have any packing tape, but duct tape will work, right?"

I nod. "Perfect. The only problem is, what are we going to attach all the posters to?"

"We can wrap the twine around the trees and then do another line along the posts on the front porch."

"Let's do it." It takes two trips to get both the posters and the scooter down the stairs, but thankfully Millie helps with all that as I hop like a bunny from step to step.

It's only the middle of the day, but the weather is cool and I grab a sweatshirt before we head outside. The actual process of taping and holding up the posters is harder than I thought it would be originally, and we have to use a lot of the duct tape to get all the posters hung up.

We finish over an hour later. I stand back and laugh. "Thanks for your help, Millie. I couldn't have done it without you."

"Well, this is the most exciting thing I've done for the past couple days. My favorite sign is 'I'm the quiet neighbor with the big freezer.' Do you think he'll like it?"

Nodding, I say, "I think he'll love it. I just hope it doesn't blow down by the time he gets here."

"I'm sure he'll be happy whenever he sees it. I'll come out and fix it if it falls down or anything." Millie gives me a small smile and grabs the tape, twine, and scissors. We walk into the house and collapse on the couch upstairs again. I left the scooter at the bottom of the stairs because I didn't want to repeat trying to get it back down again.

"Do you think there is really one person out there for everyone? A soulmate?" Millie asks, staring at the ceiling.

With a shrug, I say, "I don't know. I think that would be hard to figure out. I've gotten along with a lot of guys in life. But for one reason or another, they didn't work out. Maybe there's a soulmate for everyone, but I kind of think if there's a couple who are fantastic friends, they could make a relationship work."

"I'm a little nervous that I won't find anyone. I know I'm younger and have time for all that, but I didn't date much in high school. A couple of dances, but I've never had a boyfriend."

I reach over and pat her hands and sigh. "You might count yourself lucky then, Millie. I mean, breakups are never an easy thing. They're filled with what-could've-beens. And those last a lot longer than I want."

"Do you regret your marriage?" Millie asks. I'd told the roomies that I'd been married for all of two weeks a little over a year ago, back when Kenzie confessed to having a crush on Trey since they were in youth hockey.

Shaking my head, I say, "No, I think it was a good wake up call for me to not settle. He'd proposed almost a fake relationship situation, like Dani and Miles." We both chuckle a bit about how our former roomie and her husband got together. "I had liked the guy for months. We met in one of my classes in college. But he didn't think he could be with me because of so many reasons."

"Like what?"

"Like I hadn't come up with a new invention that could earn millions per year," I say, shaking my head at the ridiculousness of his past comments. "His family didn't think I was good enough and persuaded him to leave me for the woman they originally lined him up with. I was sick for those two weeks, too, and he looked at me like I was a burden since I wasn't doing everything for him."

Millie sits up and turns to me. "What kind of sickness?"

"I had terrible headaches and couldn't function, even doing any normal everyday things. That was only a year ago and rough. A few weeks later, my cousin was supposed to marry Hillary, and I was in my last semester of classes and clinicals to become a nurse. I had a breakdown and had to quit everything because I went blind temporarily."

"Blind?" Millie echoes. She looks shocked, which is one reason I don't tell too many people the extent of my nervous breakdown. "Do you still have problems with that?"

I shake my head. "No, I think it all happened because of stress."

"Didn't you have a lot of pressure working for that Jane lady?" Millie asks.

"Judy? Yeah, but for some reason, I could handle it. Maybe because it was on a smaller scale?" I've thought about that a lot over the past couple of days and wonder if I could've continued with nursing if I hadn't married Todd. As much as going through an annulment hurts, the lessons learned outweigh the negatives. It's worth it to hold out for someone I love and who loves me back.

"Are you hoping to date someone now? Or are you nervous about what your ex did to you?"

I smile, thinking of HuskyHiker521. "I have a pen pal and past that, I'm good right now. I mean, there's a lot to figure out just with a new career as it is. And I'm kind of hoping that if I don't go looking, I'll find someone worth spending the time on, you know?"

Millie nods. "I can understand that. For me, there's always this worry that because I didn't date much in high school, it means I've got some invisible mark that tells guys to stay away." She takes a deep breath before saying, "This doesn't even come close to what you've been through, but the guy I'd had a crush on for years finally asked me to prom my senior year. I was so excited to go and used a good chunk of my savings to purchase a dress. He ended up going with someone else. It was all a prank."

"Oh, Millie, I'm so sorry. People can be such jerks." It reminds me of the pranks I saw in my research. The not cool pranks that actually hurt people. I picture a slightly younger Millie and how crushed she'd be to get all dressed up and not have her date show.

"I've just always wondered how people get past that

liking part and finally decide to be a couple. Like, is there some magical spell we need to find to do that?"

I laugh and she joins in. "If only it were that easy."

Her words keep working through my brain as I get ready for bed later that night. I had been in the same boat as Millie through most of high school and college. I've had plenty of guy friends and I was usually included in parties and invited to activities, but that's as far as the intentions went. There were brief relationships of like two or three days, but nothing solid. I could write a book about being ghosted afterward.

I settle into bed to type out a message to HuskyHiker521, wondering what he'd have to say about his dating experiences as a male. Maybe we were all in the same boat together.

12

OWEN

I arrive at the rehab center early Monday morning, feeling more refreshed than I have in a long time. After my date with Denise Friday, working in the ER Saturday night, and a good long hike in Vermont Sunday morning, I am ready to tackle this new week.

"How's it going this morning?" I ask Susan, the woman behind the front desk at Rosewood.

"It's Monday," she says with a grumble.

"It definitely is," I say. Chances of seeing Riley now are much lower since she works the day shift. I think that's helped my blood pressure return to a normal level in my everyday life.

Susan hands me an envelope. "I think your favorite patient forgot this. The orderly was going to throw it away, but I thought I'd ask you first."

I take the envelope and see Gordon written on the front in a swoopy script. "I'll bet this is important. Thanks. I'll take it to him this afternoon."

A couple hours speed by as I visit several patients who've just arrived at the unit from the hospital and then a few of the ones I've met several times. I didn't realize how lonely some of them are until I go in and see their faces transform with excitement at my presence. There's got to be a better system of getting people to volunteer here, just to have the ones with little to no family get a visit a few times when they're here. As much as I'd like to be that visitor for all of them, there's just not enough hours in the day.

By the time it's noon, I grab the envelope and head to the address Gordon had given me before leaving the facility.

I'm not sure I'm in the right place until I see several posters strung across the lawn. Some are sagging a bit, but this must've been the latest prank by the neighbors.

As I read each one, I can't help but laugh.

WELCOME TO THE LOVE SHACK.

HONK IF YOU LIKE CATS.

DO NOT DISTURB THE GRASS. IT'S DREAMING.

YARD SALE - OUR CRAP COULD BE YOUR CRAP.

BEWARE OF SARCASM.

I'M GOING TO STAND OUTSIDE SO IF ANYONE ASKS, I AM OUTSTANDING.

I'M THE QUIET NEIGHBOR WITH THE BIG FREEZER.

I can only imagine what Gordon's face was like seeing these for the first time. Walking up to the front door, I knock.

"Come in!" a voice calls out.

Twisting the knob to the door, I push it open a couple inches and call out, "Gordon?"

"In here!"

I step inside and close the door. It smells like my grandma's always did, a bit of lemon and fresh air.

I walk around the corner and see Gordon in the recliner, a book resting on his chest.

"Owen, I didn't expect to see you so soon. This is perfect. I should be getting the materials for my next prank from the mailman today. You can help me execute it."

"It looks like you arrived home to a bunch of signs outside."

He grins. "Weren't those great? They didn't know I was gone. It makes me wonder how long the signs were up."

"What are your plans for a prank?" I'm hoping it's nothing like handling dog poop or anything gooey. I don't do well with those kinds of things unless I've got a pair of sterile gloves on. And yet I ate the shellfish the other night without a problem. I'm a conundrum even to myself.

"It's a surprise. I've been planning it for the past four days."

"What was the first prank?"

"I came outside to see an Easter invasion."

"Like eggs and bunnies?" I ask, sitting in a chair next to him.

Gordon nods. "Just like that. There were Easter signs and filled eggs throughout the yard. Troy gathered all the eggs and we found a coded message inside that it was from our neighbors."

"That's cool. It sounds like you spent a lot of time with Troy."

"Yeah, I was in hospice. They didn't think I'd live much longer. But I'm still here after six months and my last scans said my cancer has decreased in size."

I grin, imagining the fight this man has put up to still be alive. "I came to give you this."

Handing out the letter for him to take, I see the surprise in his eyes. He takes it from me and it's the first time I've seen him emotional and without a smile on his face.

"Thank you. I thought I'd lost it between the hospital

and the rehab center. It was hard to think I'd never be able to read it again."

"Is it from Vera?" I ask, curiosity getting to me.

He nods, holding it close to his chest and closing his eyes for a few moments. At one point I think he's fallen asleep.

"My Vera was a treasure. I had been dating a few women when I met her. We became friends through a service group we both attended. After a time, I realized I didn't want anyone but her. She was definitely worth all the bumps in the road to get to her."

Giving Gordon a warm smile, I nod. "That's amazing. I'm not sure stuff like that happens these days."

"You can't give up so easily, son. You'll find your girl in the most random of circumstances." He pauses a moment and says, "I think that's the mail carrier. Maybe my package came."

He waves for me to go get the package at the front door.

"What's in here?" I ask, walking back with a medium-sized box.

Gordon's mischievous grin makes me laugh. "Caution tape."

"What?" That was the last thing I expected to hear.

"We're going to make it look like a crime was committed at their house."

"I don't know if that's a good idea," I say, trying to figure out how I got stuck in a situation like this. Is that even legal? I don't need to be arrested for impersonating an officer.

Gordon waves a hand to brush away my words and says, "It will be great. I'll just need your help to take the tape and wrap it around the house. I also got some chalk, so we can do an outline of a body."

"Who are we going to outline?" I ask, wondering if I can

escape before taking part in this. I did agree to help him when he was at the center.

"We'll have to find someone outside walking around and ask them. Let's get started now. The girls are all gone during the day."

"Are you sure there isn't another prank we can do?"

"Let's go," Gordon says, trying to push up out of the chair.

"I don't know if it's good for you to be on your leg for an extended amount of time. Hobbling around the yard is too much."

Gordon shakes his head. "Oh, I won't be doing that," he says, pushing the box toward me.

"What if someone sees us?"

"Don't you know how to have fun, Owen? This is fun. It's where you do something that brings a smile to your face even after it's all over."

Guilt pricks at me. Have I really become that much of a bore that an eighty-one-year-old is calling me out?

"I'll help for ten minutes and that's it."

Gordon looks as though he's just won the lottery. "Perfect. I'll take whatever we can get."

Blowing out a breath, I take the tape from him and help him into the wheelchair next to his seat. We make it out to the porch and I lock the wheels so he doesn't go cruising into the flower bed while I'm playing a prank. As a twenty-eight-year-old. In broad daylight.

There are several trees next to the sidewalk and I start there, wrapping the bright yellow tape around each one and continuing onto the next. I travel up to the front porch and start wrapping it around the first post but there is a light on inside.

I duck down as I see a figure walk in the room with the light on. Did they see me?

Why am I worried about getting caught? If this has been going on for several months, they probably aren't surprised about anything that happens out here.

I stand up again and wrap from one post to the other, closing off the path that leads off the porch and to the street. Once I've made the full loop, I walk back over to Gordon, checking my watch. How did that only take four minutes and fifty-five seconds?

He grins and hands me a box of chalk. "Go get 'em, Tiger."

I give him the smallest of smiles and try to figure out how to draw a dead body without something to trace. Art has never been my forte. To be honest, my penmanship isn't readable, so that should explain a lot.

The chalk box is filled with colors like red, blue, green, and yellow, but no white. So it won't look just like a crime scene scenario. Instead, I get an idea and start drawing. I'm so invested now that even when the timer goes off, I ignore it. I've used up all the red pieces of chalk and outlined the character in green with x-ed out eyes.

"Did you kill Santa?" a voice asks, and I turn to see a small girl with big wide eyes standing next to me.

"Um, no. This is all just a joke. I was just drawing for fun," I say, glancing around as I try to find her parents.

"But that looks like Santa, only his beard is blue."

I'm working hard to come up with some story. The girl has to be around seven years old. When do kids find out about a certain man's identity? Never mind, I don't want to be the one to ruin dreams.

"This is Santa's lesser-known brother. His name is Sid

and every time he does something wrong, his beard turns blue."

The little girl is watching the scene as if trying to decide if I'm right. I glance past her and see a familiar face in the window of the house. Great, can I just buy a ticket to anywhere but here and disappear?

Evie Evans is Gordon's neighbor? Or maybe she's just visiting someone.

"I'll have to do some research," the girl says, skipping away.

As soon as she rounds the corner to the yard on the other side of the house I've just pranked, I scramble to pick up every piece of chalk, throwing them into the cardboard box. It rips on the one side and the chalk falls back to the sidewalk with several small clinks. A few pieces break and I repeat the process, hoping the face I saw in the window wasn't actually Evie.

"Are you following me?" Evie asks. I jump at her voice because she's either a cat with her scooter or I was so focused on the chalk that I didn't hear her approach.

"No, definitely not." My hands are completely covered in chalk with all the colors possible in the box. I scowl down at them, needing to get the feel of it off.

"Are you working with my neighbor?" Evie asks, holding onto her handlebars.

I give her a curt nod. "Gordon and I met a couple of weeks ago. But this is my first time working on a prank here."

"Gordon is his name. Thank you."

I frown again, wondering what she means. "You didn't know your neighbor's name? Aren't you the one who started all this?" I ask, waving my arms around to the caution tape and the awful picture of Santa's brother.

She's looking over at the house next door and waves. Instead of answering my question, she rolls her scooter over the dead outline of Sid Claus and makes her way past me on the sidewalk, heading over to where Gordon is still parked on the porch.

I take a few extra seconds to react and she's next to him by the time I run across the lawn.

"Gordon, I'm Evie Evans. I live next door." She leans in a bit closer and says, "I'm the prank instigator. I have to say that you have come up with some of the best pranks. Police tape? That was genius."

Gordon's grin is wider than anything I've seen from him over the past hour. "It's nice to meet the legend of the Next-Door Prankster."

Evie laughs too, shifting to sit on her scooter. I want to say something about that not being good for her foot, but there's only so much I can say. I'm more mesmerized by the interaction between the two of them. Evie is so relaxed compared to the past few times we've met.

"My roommates still talk about the giant pool animals."

"Troy helped a lot. He'd make sure I was his last patient of the day so he could spend some extra time helping me with it." His smile drops and he glances down at his hands.

"But it sounds like you're the brain of the operation. Do you miss Troy?" Evie asks.

Gordon nods, and I feel like I'm interrupting some intimate conversation.

"Well, it might take some coaxing for this guy," Evie says, jutting her thumb in my direction. "If you can get him to smile longer than five seconds, I'd put it in as some kind of miracle."

I try to smile, but instead I'm frustrated over what she's saying. "I smile."

She grins and raises an eyebrow. "I've known you for less than a couple of days, and I've only seen a hint that the corners of your lips turn upward." Something about her words must have hit her because she turns back toward Gordon, but not before I see the tips of her ears turning bright red. Was it the fact that she's been watching for those little details?

"I've had a lot of life adjustments lately. There's no way you can smile all day every day."

"True. But I do have a lot to be grateful for."

It's my turn to raise an eyebrow. "Like your job?"

She frowns. "Don't remind me about that." Evie shifts to her kneeling position on the scooter and says, "I should probably get back so I can rest my leg, but it was so nice to meet you, Gordon."

"You too, Evie. I'm excited to see what you come up with next." I'm pretty sure I've never seen someone get so excited about pranks. I avoided them completely growing up. They usually involve a mess, and I can't handle being wet or sticky for long periods of time.

Maybe I am a grump. I'll just have to show Evie this is a temporary personality quirk.

Not that she is the only one who needs that PSA.

13

EVIE

I probably shouldn't have ragged on Owen in front of Gordon. But the guy could use a week-long vacation on a beach in the Bahamas to loosen up a bit.

I've checked my messages at least four times in the past hour, wondering when HuskyHiker will grace me with a message. The more I think about it, the more I'm curious about how guys are. I mean, I only have two brothers to use data from, but they are so wildly different that I don't feel like I have a clear definition of them.

What are the chances Owen is friends with my neighbor? He wasn't in scrubs, so he had to be there on a friendly visit.

The two of them are an odd pair. Gordon is like the sunshine personality, and Owen is more like Eeyore, with the dark clouds over him all the time.

I spend the next couple of days over-analyzing everything I've done in my life until this point. I've applied for a few different jobs and studied some patterns for robes and memory bears so I can make a few testers. Ruining people's treasured memories while I'm testing things out would haunt me for life.

But the new shop across town isn't hiring, and I don't want the pressure of actually planning a wedding. I know the stress will only be a repeat of what happened during clinicals, and I don't want to completely ruin another career choice for myself. Then again, it feels like I already have.

I think back to when my life changed so drastically. I'd woken up one morning after a stressful week and no matter how many appointments I had, they weren't able to figure out what the cause of my symptoms was. Withdrawing from nursing school when I was so close to the end wrecked me and I cried for days. But what was worse was the fact I didn't know when or if I would regain my sight.

Three weeks after it first happened, I slowly got my sight back. To say I'm extra grateful for my sight now is an understatement.

One thing that rang true through it all is that the man I marry needs to handle all things health-wise without running away. When I was with Todd, I just had a constant headache and he freaked out. He would've died had I been blind while we were together. Having to take care of me instead of me doing everything to make him comfortable would've sent him straight home to his parents' house.

Do I tell HuskyHiker any of this? It seems like a big, personal thing, which is what we avoid in our messages. But after getting to know him through the letters, I think he could keep those kinds of secrets and understand them.

The doctors attributed everything to being overly stressed, so I'm on a low-stress diet now. The nice thing is I can be the supportive character in my roommates' lives while feeling like I've learned something. It's almost like reading different genres of books. I live vicariously through them and their drama.

Rachelle getting back with her ex-fiancé, Landon, on a cruise. I missed a lot of that one because I wasn't on the cruise, but I was definitely there post-breakup. Dani falling for Miles, her fake fiancé. Yeah, that one stressed me out. I mean, I visibly sweat when I'm trying to lie, so I would've looked like I'd taken a shower with all my clothes on every time I had to pretend anything.

And Kenzie. Her happily-ever-now moments with Trey are worth all the twisting of the heartstrings that happened for them to actually get together. She made a joke that the roommates were all going to match up with the friend group. That's a definite no. I'd probably strangle Jack on our first date and Spencer feels like a little brother, if I were to ever have one.

So, I safely type about random things to my pen pal and call that good when it comes to relationships with the opposite sex.

I've made it five days with a boot on and the scooter. At least it coincides with the time when I don't have to go to work every day.

My phone rings and I grin as I see my sister-in-law's name on the caller ID.

"Hey Tiff, how are you?"

"I am desperate. I need to head into work for about two hours today to talk to the contractor about our remodel next door. Meg is out of town and Drew is dealing with a flooding issue in one of the apartment buildings. Is there any way you can watch Ellie Jo? Today is your day off, right?"

I don't mean to laugh, but I can't help but think about what happened the last time I babysat. Then again, my niece isn't old enough to need constant entertainment.

"Sure. Do you mind bringing her here? I've got a lot going on today and that will help me stay on top of things." In reality, I just don't want to traipse through Boston with my new wheely appendage.

"Perfect."

Tiffany is at our door in record time and walks in with a car seat holding my adorable niece and a backpack that could rival Mary Poppins' bag.

"What happened to your yard? Why is there a yellow tape ev—" she says, stopping when she sees me. "What happened to you? Did you get hurt outside and that's why there's police tape?"

I laugh, shaking my head. The other roomies have been too busy to take the tape down and I haven't had the energy to even think about it. I focus on taking Ellie Jo out of her car seat before sharing the details of my broken foot.

"Why didn't you call me? I would've helped you get anywhere you need to go."

"I'm fine. I don't have to worry about getting too many places."

Tiffany looks skeptical. "What about work? Do you take a car to get there every day?"

I give her a sad smile and say, "I actually quit a few days ago. Judy made me try on a dress and then was going to charge me the full price because a couple of beads came off."

Tiffany gasps. "Girl, I need to come over more often to get all this gossip. I can't believe all that happened just this week. We've had the flu, and I feel like I've missed all the things."

"Please tell me you're not still sick," I say, laughing. "I don't need to get more doctor bills through the mail." I've gotten one from the hospital so far, and luckily my meager insurance covered that part.

"No, we've been over it for the last several days. Thank you again for your help with Ellie Jo." She gives me a run-down on the baby's needs and feeding times and heads out.

Baby girl fusses a bit, and I rock her gently. She's such a sweet thing and juts out her bottom lip as she settles back to sleep in my arms. We sit on the big couch and I turn on one of my favorite shows, an older one that's black and white. My roommates don't get the attraction of liking a film made in the past century, but there's something classic about those kinds. And I can't refuse a good romance with a happily ever after that makes me melt a bit. Even if the chances of it happening to me are slim.

My phone pings and I see the symbol of the Love, Austen app at the top of my screen. I rarely get notifications from there and I'm hoping it's not because I've been paired up. I'm not at a place where a relationship would be benefi-cial. Every time I think back to my last one, all I can think about is how Todd reacted to everything about me in the end. Is it possible to find a guy who'll put aside his assump-tions and love me for who I am on the app?

I swipe down to see the short recap of what the message says. It rarely comes up like that when HuskyHiker sends me a message.

HH: Are you online right now? I thought I saw your light was available and figured we could chat more now.

Me: I'm here.

How lame can I get? And why am I feeling so flustered when talking to him? Maybe it's because when I message on my own terms, I can relegate him to the realm of brotherly friends in my mind. Instant messaging feels way more inti-mate than an email buddy.

HH: How are you doing?

How do I answer that? Counting pennies since I lost my job. Trying to keep any shred of dignity after obliterating my foot in a child's game. I'm on a roll.

But the excitement over my sewing projects bubbles to the surface again, and I feel good about it. The hardest part will be figuring out how to advertise my services. Website? Social Media? Ads?

I glance down at the sleeping baby in my arms and smile. There's something so peaceful about my little niece and there's a minor ache in my chest, probably because I'd love to be a mother, but I've been thinking about what Millie said the other day. How do you go from liking someone to being in a relationship without scaring the person away?

Me: Good. Tired but good. I'm holding a sleeping baby, so that's always a good thing.

There are several dots popping up and then they disappear, only to show up again a few seconds later. It makes me wonder what he's trying to type out.

HH: Did you find a baby on the street? Or are you related to him/her?

Me: Haha. She's my niece. I'm babysitting for a couple hours.

HH: *sends meme of Matthew McConaughey saying "Gotcha"*

Me: Were you worried?

At least a minute goes by before he answers.

HH: I was curious. I mean, we've never shared anything major from our personal life. I figure we should probably check on a few things. Are you married?

I blink a few times and wonder why we're suddenly leaping into a very personal topic. How do I answer that? Do

I tell him I was married once upon a time for a brief stint, but now I'm single and not so ready to mingle?

Not that I've been on scores of dates, but after I reveal the divorce card, it's like everyone starts looking for the flaws that drove me to that point.

Me: No. Not married. I was once for a couple weeks, but it didn't work out. What about you?

Now we've gone way past a casual pen pal. We're delving into secrets that I didn't think I'd have to share with Husky-Hiker. At least not for the next year, at the rate we were going.

When he doesn't answer, I turn off the screen and try to focus on the show.

It's official. I'm a social pariah with a big letter D tattooed to my forehead.

Ellie Jo moves and she gives an enormous yawn before settling back into the warmth of her blanket. What would it be like to be responsible full-time for a thing so small?

My brain is trying to forget about HuskyHiker. Maybe we can go back to our conversations and not worry about the fact that I'm damaged goods. Well, not really. More like returned after being taken out of the box.

Todd never wanted to know the real me, and I was too gone on him to notice that, using my people pleasing capabilities in full force to keep our relationship together.

And of course, karma swoops in as I am thinking about it all and my tears start to spill right as the kissing scene in the movie occurs.

"What's wrong, Evie?" Millie asks from the stairs. I can see her hair bouncing through the railing as she jogs upstairs.

I try to pull back all the tears I spilt and wipe away at my cheeks. "Nothing. I'm good."

Millie takes a seat next to me but she turns, angling her body toward me, meaning we're going to have to have this conversation. She's got one eyebrow raised when she says, "I don't think you are. Talk to Millikins."

Her nickname makes me laugh, breaking the sad moment I just went through. "Do you get called that often?" I ask, hoping to stall as I slowly push the emotions behind a wall. Too bad the wall is made of tissue paper that probably won't make it through the next five minutes.

"Yeah, that's what my family called me as a kid. Sometimes I hate it, because I feel like I haven't grown out of that stage, but other times it reminds me of home."

I nod. "That's got to be hard. Any luck in the job department?"

She shakes her head. "But we're not talking about me at the moment. You've done so much for me. The least I can do is be a listening ear."

Breathing deeply, I let the air go slowly, trying to order my thoughts somewhat. "I am just in a weird headspace today. I don't know if it's because I don't currently have a job, or if it's because of ninety-nine other problems."

"What started it?"

My pen pal. I don't want to say that, though. Maybe it's time I address all the things I've tucked away so well. It's practically an Evans trait, the avoidance and pretending things are just fine.

"I don't know. I've always had goals for myself and it's like I'm failing every. Single. One. lately. It's discouraging, you know?" I let myself mope for a moment and then remember the bear that's almost done on my sewing table downstairs.

Millie nods. "For sure. I've felt like that, the past week

especially. It used to happen to me a lot when we'd go hiking during hunting season and not find any wildlife for the several days we were out."

I frown. Does everyone in the world hike but me? Maybe I should introduce Millie to HuskyHiker521. Because there's got to be some reason he picked that as his username. Then again, I picked mine to ward off the crazy intense guys. So maybe I've got it all wrong.

"One thing my mom has always told me is that sometimes it seems like the world is against everything you want or need. But you have to go through those hard experiences to understand and better appreciate it when you get the things you've dreamed of. So something great is going to come on the horizon."

"So the more mishaps and trouble I go through, the better the payoff later? That sounds counterproductive," I say. Mentally, I kick myself. I'm usually overly optimistic about everything. Right now, I'm just trying to stay afloat.

Millie shrugs. "I know it sounds strange, but I think it's all about the attitude, you know? Kind of turn the frown upside down and all that. Saying things out loud helps a lot, too."

"Are you just saying that so I'll spill my secrets?" I say, trying to keep a teasing tone in my voice. I lean my head back on the couch cushion and stare up at the ceiling.

"I mean, if you want to share, I'm here. I might be sheltered in the real world, but I can share whatever little advice I have that might help."

She's already making sense. But does my stubborn mind want to give in or just close up like the fireworks displays on July 5th?

"I have a pen pal."

Millie squeals next to me and claps her hands together. "That's so fun. Tell me everything."

Her enthusiasm causes a part of the fear inside me to loosen. "We met on the Love, Austen app, messaging for a few weeks now and it's been casual, platonic stuff. We weren't supposed to share anything personal. And tonight he messaged me about a bunch of personal stuff and I told him I was once married." Lifting my phone up, I say, "And now he's gone radio silent."

"It's possible he had to do something. What if his house was on fire? He'd have to call the fire department and try to get the flames to go away before messaging you again."

I raise an eyebrow and laugh. "I don't know. It's too coincidental."

"What if he's just been through something similar? Maybe it triggered him?" Millie looks at me like a sad puppy. "That would be awful, though."

I nod, agreeing with her there. "I don't think that helps make things better."

We're both silent for a few moments and I try to shift so the baby is resting more on the couch than my arm, which is going numb.

My phone pings and I know I look like I'm crazy when I swipe open to see what it's for. Sagging back into the cushions, I close my eyes.

"Not your pen pal?" Millie asks.

"It was a text for a company I subscribed to to get a discount from. Of all the times for them to send a text."

Millie laughs. "Sounds about right. But that might make his answer even better when it comes in." She stands, and I'm kind of sad to see her go. While our conversation wouldn't be recorded in any published journals, it was comforting, or at least taking my mind off the messages.

This is why I don't get involved. I overanalyze to the point of insanity.

"I need to take a shower. I had to help Beau and Spencer clean out some warehouse they're going to rent for their company."

"Is your brother planning to stick around for longer than a week?" I ask, surprised at this turn of events. Granted, I'd only met him when in severe pain, but he seemed like a nice guy.

Millie shrugs. "We never know with Beau. He's one of those 'blown everywhere by whims and winds', as my father would say."

I smile and think about that as she disappears into the bathroom. These past few years, I've felt pushed and blown to different areas of life than I thought I'd be. But maybe what Millie said is true. I just need to wait for the payoff of all the crazy while keeping a good attitude about it. I rarely have to work too hard for that, but the strikes are against me, pressing down on me like I'm a walking tic-tac-toe board just waiting for the O to block me.

Another ping from my phone has me more calmly turning on the screen. It's the little daisy at the top.

HH: Recent breakup, but no weddings. I can't imagine what it would be like to go through all that. My father left when I was young, but I didn't even realize it for a few weeks. Mom was everything to us.

Relief pours through me that he hasn't completely ghosted me. And even though I've been against sharing personal things in the past month, I can understand the shift that happens when I learn little things about him.

Could this turn into something more? Possibly.

If only we could speed through the awkward parts in a few weeks. I smile, thinking how every humiliating moment has been in front of Owen these past couple weeks. And yet, it's almost like he's softening toward me.

Maybe we'll end up friends yet.

14

OWEN

I'm a complete disaster of a person. If there was a way to go back in time at least fifteen minutes, I'd do it.

I don't know what I was thinking of asking so many personal questions to TheWeddingPlanner2. The one rule she'd stated from the beginning of our written relationship was that we'd keep things casual, talk more about ideas than concrete things in our life. I've crossed that line and I don't know if we're coming back from it.

And yet, I still file away the bit of information that she's been married, even for a short stint, in my brain. Part of me wonders what the circumstances were for her split. It's possible it was all her fault and she's the problem. But from everything I've learned from her, I think it was her partner. Not that it matters.

Hopefully, I didn't scare her away. Because through the mess of the past several weeks, I've had two constants, TheWeddingPlanner2 and Gordon Attenbury. Both have been able to get me through this breakup by just being there and listening. Sure, I haven't shared any of my breakup with my pen pal, except that it was recent, but the benefit of typing things on a phone or computer is the lack of pitying glances.

That's probably why I'm struggling right now.

I had to accept Jack's proposal to go to the movies. The guy is persistent and doesn't take no for an answer. Little did I know this would be like an intervention at the movies when the rest of the guy group shows up, Beau included.

"You'll be fine, man," and "We'll just have to line you up with someone else" are pretty much their only narrative since arriving. At least I'm full of extra buttered popcorn and a soda. Which means I have to go to the bathroom only twenty minutes into the show.

It's okay. We're just watching the twentieth sequel in a car heist franchise. I've got the plot down.

So instead of going right back in, I find a bench and decide to check messages. There's no way I can do that in front of the guys. They'll be all over me about when the wedding will be and why haven't we met in person yet?

I'm surprised TheWeddingPlanner2 is online and it feels different knowing she's present while we're talking.

TheWeddingPlanner2: No. Not married. I was once for a couple of weeks, but it didn't work out. What about you?

And then I remember that we'd talked about that before. So much for my brain keeping everything important in its vault.

There are a host of scenarios that play out across my mind. One is that she could be a serial killer and that's the reason they were only married for a couple of weeks.

No, that's a big leap.

Maybe the guy embezzled money from his company and was put behind bars, leading her to get a divorce.

Or she could've just had the opposite of what I went through. That's the most logical choice.

Me: Recent breakup, but no weddings. I can't imagine what it would be like to go through all that. My father left when I was young, but I didn't even realize it for a few weeks. Mom was everything to us.

And there I go again, making it even worse. We've turned a corner and I can't go back to the way things were before. Then again, maybe that's what I need.

I've been hiding ever since Riley broke up with me, tending to my wounds like a dog after getting stuck in a bear trap. Not that I want anything different, but if my pen pal lives in the same city as me, why not be able to meet up and chat in person?

TheWeddingPlanner2: My mother was amazing too. At least from what I can remember of her. My father loves me in his own way, but it's not an outright deal.

I tap my fingers on my leg, trying to figure out where to go from here.

It sounds like we have a lot more than travel in common.

Me: Do you want to meet up?

It takes at least thirty seconds of me holding my breath as I try to figure out if I should send it. Then I delete and retype it.

Blowing out a breath, I push the little paper airplane icon to send it. Instead of waiting for the answer, I tuck my phone into my pants pocket and head back into the movie. It will keep me in suspense for the rest of the show, but in some strange way, it gives me an excitement I haven't had in a long time.

By the time we leave the theater, though, there isn't a response. Maybe she fell asleep, or the baby is crying and she's got to take care of the little one.

Or she thinks that's the worst idea in the world.

It isn't until I get home and change for bed that I get a response.

TheWeddingPlanner2: Give me some more time.

No, it's not the answer I want, but at least it's not an outright no. Meeting might break our relationship completely. I don't need to ruin that lifeline right now.

15

EVIE

I've been tempted to delete the Love, Austen app from my phone for the past twelve hours. We've only been messaging each other for a few months at this point and I had visions of us continuing this until my hands were wrinkled and I had coke-bottle glasses. That would be a romantic story, just not the happily ever after at the end.

He wants to meet? Why?

Me: Give me some more time.

I can only think that maybe he wants to see if I'm a troll or something before he keeps contacting me.

I know how it feels to be waiting for an answer. Cue the footage of my near-freak out with Millie playing my therapist. That's why I left my answer open-ended.

And now I'm going to fully focus on the task ahead—the next prank for Gordon. I found several great options for pranks, but many will have to wait until I'm employed again for me to afford buying things, even at the not-a-dollar-anymore store.

That's another reason for the fervor I have for working on this prank. I've finished two memory bears and I'm kind of stuck where to go from here. Luke says I need to build a presence online, so while I work on that, I need something to occupy my mind.

I found enough coinage under couch cushions and in the laundry room to buy three packages of plastic forks. Too bad someone hasn't invented a glow-in-the-dark fork. That would make this prank the best to see at night.

Yes, I'm wheeling around Gordon's yard on my scooter, leaning over at intervals to press the ends of the forks into the ground. I used the last piece of posterboard I had to write, "You've been forked!" on it.

Gordon has kept all the other signs up. Well, I'm sure he asked Owen to move them to the front porch, where they are now turned so Gordon can read them from the window. That's what I'm guessing, anyway. I don't want to ask too many questions and have the magic of this prank battle ruined.

The brisk fall wind is cutting through my puffy coat and nicer gloves. But I've only got another box to go before I can go home and cuddle up in my cozy bed.

This having a broken foot thing is making me more like a hermit than normal. Probably because my knee is sore from kneeling on the scooter for so long and I don't want to go anywhere because of it.

I turn my focus to the things I can control. An email came in earlier today informing me I have a Zoom interview tomorrow morning for a wedding supply company. That's something.

I loved taking some of my mother's old clothes and making the memory bear. There have to be people out there who would benefit from this. I just need to track them down.

My thoughts turn to my mother's wedding dress hanging

in my old closet at my dad's house. I've thought of getting it and trying out a few things with it. But there's so much emotion around it that I don't want to cut it up to try to repurpose it.

I might be able to find a dress at a thrift store, though. It wouldn't even have to be white. I could practice with a piece that people already threw away. The thrift store will go on my list for tomorrow. I smile as I think about it. I have a plan. It's simple, but I'm excited about it.

Once I've finished forking the grass, I wheel my squeaky scooter back home and sneak into my bedroom before any of the others can see me come in. I pick up the memory bear with pastels from my mother's collection. There's one for Drew and Luke, with another set cut out to make one for me.

I wrap up in my sheet and comforter, holding onto the bear. Typically, I don't keep my socks and sweatshirt on in bed, but I need to warm up a bit. With my laptop open in front of me, I search for websites that people offer their sewing services on.

After two hours of research, I make a folder for everything I've sewn and tailored. It takes some time to find and add a few of the pictures past clients have sent me wearing their beautiful gowns.

Prank done and information organized in a file folder. I'm on fire.

The hardest part is the actual website. I know my limits. Who can I ask for help with that? My technical skills have been maxed out on searching the internet part. I don't know where to start with setting up code or figuring out the right file sizes.

Miles is a businessman. Maybe he'll know a thing or two about websites. Kenzie has a site for her organizational business, but I can't remember if she created it or if she had someone else help her. Beau and Spencer might be options as well, since they're starting their own production company.

I make a list to ask any of them if they can help me with this. Then I spend the time going through all the classifieds on Imagebooks, looking for anyone who's asked about having something tailored in the past couple of weeks and commenting on it.

By the time I fall asleep, it's nearly midnight and my brain is completely exhausted from the research. But it feels so good to have taken steps to move forward, rather than moping.

My mind won't shut off. It doesn't help that I'm still stuck on HuskyHiker wanting to meet. I'm not good with the center of attention energy. That was always my brother, Luke's, domain.

I'll just have to continue writing to him like nothing happened.

16

OWEN

I t's Thursday before I visit Gordon again. I make the excuse that I want to check on his leg and make sure the wound is healing well, even though he has a home health nurse that comes and checks on it periodically. In reality, I'm still trying to wade through my conscious brain, and being around Gordon helps in so many ways.

"So, your pen pal didn't want to meet up, huh?"

I shake my head, taking in a deep breath before saying, "Not necessarily. She just said she needs more time before an in-person meeting."

"What if she's got a large lump on her back and has to have it removed before you think of her as the Hunchback of Notre Dame?" Gordon asks, wiggling his eyes with the jab.

"I don't think that's the case, Gordon. Maybe she's just been through a lot in the past. She said she was married for a short period, so that could be code for she needs time to work through that." I rub my hand over my face and say, "But I'm not looking for a relationship either. Okay, not so much a romantic one. I'd meet up with her for a drink or coffee and we could catch up on each other's lives."

Gordon nods a few times. "If you become good friends with her and eventually find someone to date and then marry," he says, giving me a look to bear with him when he sees I'm getting impatient, "chances are high that your new lady won't be happy about you having a good friend who's a woman."

Taking a deep breath, I say, "So you think I should just break off the writing now before anything develops further?"

"No, absolutely not. I think you just need to be aware of that."

I mull over his words and work to get my thoughts to all line up. "You're right. And I don't know why I'm worried about it right now. It's like meeting anyone. We don't have any romantic attachments right now. I just thought it would be nice to talk to her online and in person if she lives in the city."

"That's understandable. But have patience, Young Padawan."

I chuckle at his Star Wars reference. It was a series I loved growing up. And in a sense, I feel a lot like Luke Skywalker talking to Yoda, minus the whining and need to practice fighting. Okay, maybe I'm whining, but not much.

"I went on a date the other night. She works at the hospital." Why am I mentioning my date with Denise? I haven't thought about her since I dropped her off.

Gordon's eyebrows raise. "Dating a coworker. Isn't that frowned on?"

Shaking my head, I say, "Kind of, but not really. My ex-girlfriend and I worked the same shift. She moved to the day shift when she broke up with me. Which is nice, so I don't have to see her every time I work."

"What made you go on the date?" Gordon asks.

With a shrug, I say, "My sister, Darcy, said I should go on a revenge date. Basically, to go on a date with a woman to make my ex jealous."

"Did it work?" Gordon asks.

"I don't know. I think I'm at the point where I don't care if it does or not. I don't want her back and there will be no date number two with my coworker."

Gordon smiles. "Don't rush it. You'll be fine. And pen pal gal will meet you at some point. It's inevitable." He pauses for a moment before saying, "I have another prank I can use your help with. Do you have some time to help me set it up?"

Shaking my head, I say, "How much time are we talking? Hopefully this isn't like the last one. I almost blew a big secret about Santa for a young girl."

"We are setting up a treasure hunt. If you'll go look on the kitchen table, I've got a small treasure chest that arrived yesterday."

"What did you put inside it?" I ask as I walk over to where he directed.

"Nothing yet," he calls. I grab it and bring it back to him. "But we'll add a fun surprise. I've got a few ideas of where we can lead them. It will start with a small clue and then they'll have to figure out the next from there until they get to the tree where the box will be hiding."

I laugh. "Are you sure you don't want to make it a buried treasure?"

Gordon taps his lips with his fingers and says, "That's a great idea. I'll just have to change that last clue."

"I shouldn't have said anything. You're going to make me dig a hole now, aren't you?"

He grins at me and nods.

We spend the next hour working out where all the clues are supposed to go and then writing them on cream paper. Gordon uses his cursive skills to make it look a lot like the old lettering from an eighteenth-century treasure hunt. He even insists we burn the edges of each piece to make it look authentic.

He directs me where to find a shovel, and I dig a hole next to the fence that adjoins Evie's house. It's in a spot of dirt already, which is easier than trying to pull up the grass, especially since there are forks everywhere. But it's dry and it feels like I'm bending the head of the shovel with every movement.

"How did you get so many ideas of what to do for your pranks?" I ask, lifting a shovel full of dirt. It's difficult enough for him to use his phone, let alone use the internet to search for things. Then again, he's fantastic at online shopping.

"I go back through all the movies I've seen and use those ideas to spin off new ones."

"So, the crime scene was from a movie?"

He nods and laughs. "You look like I just told you your puppy died. There are a lot of ways to tweak ideas to work for this situation."

Once the hole is dug, I place the small treasure chest in it and fill it back in, trying to make it look like the rest of the garden. I even dig around in other garden areas in Gordon's yard to hopefully throw them off. Call it my own tweak to Gordon's prank.

Gordon uses a wheelchair to follow me around as we "plant" all the clues, several of them in the neighbors' yard, which means I have to be more discreet than the last prank we pulled.

After planting all but one clue, I'm instructed to hold a box with the first clue and knock on the ladies' door. I'd argued plenty that this was Gordon's prank and he should be the one to start it off, but he just shakes his head and laughs from the front porch.

I stand in front of the door, feeling an odd mix of dread and excitement at the thought of pulling this off. Sure, this might not seem like the greatest prank, but what's inside the box makes it worth it.

The door swings open and a young woman with red hair stands there. She gives me an odd look and then glances down at the box. She looks familiar. After a few moments, I finally connect that she was with Evie at the ER the night she came in.

"Are you selling something?" she asks.

I shake my head. "No, I'm just delivering this package from your neighbor next door."

That seems to help her click things into place. She turns around and calls out, "Evie. Your next prank awaits."

The way she says it makes me think I'm here to ask Evie out to prom or something. And with surprising speed given the scooter, Evie arrives at the door, all smiles until she sees me there.

"Are you supposed to be the prank?" she says, letting the corner of her mouth hitch up a fraction of an inch. Her intense brown eyes are on me, and all I can think about is that I'm struck by how beautiful she is. I haven't taken the time to look at her like this, although I need to push that to the side and move on. Gordon will tease me that I spent too much time over here.

"Partially, yes," I say, trying to make my voice nonchalant. "This is for you. Gordon says your treasure hunt awaits."

Evie takes the box from me, our hands barely brushing, and I'm surprised by the connection I feel there. Or it could be the fact that I'm in recovery from not having slept normally for almost two weeks. Yep, I'll go with that.

She pops the lid open, and I turn to leave. With a quick glance over at Gordon, I give him a thumbs up and walk toward him. The guy is just as excited as Evie to do this.

It makes me think through all my decisions the past year. I've been so serious about life, having to push to make more money and follow along as Riley tried to get our lives to the next level, whatever that means. But the simplicity of having fun, of laughing even, shouldn't be a luxury that comes once in a blue moon.

Jack was right. I need to loosen up. A few pranks are sure to do that.

17

EVIE

I'm surprised Mr. Grumpy Owen would willingly take part in another prank. It makes me wonder what kind of relationship he has with Gordon. Maybe he's a distant nephew and just takes time to hang out with the older man. Then again, Gordon had some bandages around his leg the last time I saw him outside, so maybe Owen is a home nurse for him or something.

I focus my attention on the white box and the small slip of paper inside. It's incredible the detail that was put into this. The edges of the paper are burned and the writing is swoopy and almost hard to read. Now I feel bad that I haven't taken as much time to create my designs. Is this supposed to be a competition?

Shaking my head, I know Gordon is just happy to have someone doing something fun for him. I don't see the home health people coming as often now, and I wonder if a prank battle has helped his health somehow. That's probably reaching, but it would be a cool story.

"What does the clue say?" Millie asks over my shoulder.

"Search ye must for the long-lost treasure of Attenbury.

Begin the quest at the side of the house, where the roses have never bloomed."

Laughing, I work my scooter down the few steps on the porch and head to the driveway. There's a small garden with bushes there that are supposed to be roses. They haven't bloomed since I moved in last spring.

Then I think about Owen having to come over and hide this. Did he come over for all the clues? No, he wasn't tromping into my room, but I've been home all day. He must be good at keeping things uber quiet.

The next clue is in a similar small box and I hand the other one to Millie, saying, "Keep this. I'm sure I'll use it in the future."

Clue after clue takes us around the entire outside of our house and then over to Gordon's yard. The clue tells us to take a shovel from the garage and head to the dirt pile.

There are several of those on his property.

"Over there looks like it was recently dug up," Millie says, taking the shovel for me. I'm sure I would've looked lady-like trying to dig it up while staying balanced on the scooter.

We dig for several minutes to realize this might not be the right spot.

Chuckling comes on the wind to us and I turn to see Gordon and Owen on the porch.

"You're in the wrong spot, my dear," Gordon says, laughing. "That was a good idea, Owen. We've really tricked them."

I glare at Owen, knowing he probably made it worse on purpose. But then again, he had to dig up all the dry areas, so joke's on him.

"By the fence?" Millie asks in a soft voice out of the corner of her mouth.

I turn slowly to see another spot that looks to be recently disturbed. "Let's try it."

Now I feel bad I can't help Millie when this is from the trouble I've caused starting the pranks. Then again, Millie is just as excited trying to figure out where all the clues are as I am.

It doesn't take as long this time since there isn't a dry hard spot underneath the layer of topsoil like the other area, so she keeps digging and hits onto something hard.

We look at each other and grin. I know it's childish, but to have gone on a fun little treasure hunt hits a dream I didn't know I had.

Millie pulls out a box and brushes off a lot of the dirt. It's a mini treasure chest and I can't stop smiling. There is a small latch that I have to push and the top springs back, revealing another piece of paper inside.

I open it and read, "The biggest treasure is the adventure." I tip my head back and laugh long and loud. It's better than anything else that could've been in the box.

"What do you think?" Gordon asks.

I wheel myself through the bumpy grass, avoiding several of the forks that are still standing up along the way. "I think this was the perfect prank."

"Why thank you. I'm the brains of the operation, but the grunt work was all done by this guy." Gordon slaps Owen's back and chuckles.

Owen shrugs, giving him a minimal smile. "At least you gave me some credit. I wondered if you were going to say you did it all."

"I'm good, but not that good."

We all laugh at that.

"I guess I have some planning to do for the next round of

this game," I say, reaching out to give the treasure box to Gordon.

He waves his hands in front of it and says, "It's yours. Keep it."

"Thank you. I'm sure I'll figure out a way to use it in the future." I give him a quick wink and say, "Okay, good luck, boys. Stay out of trouble."

"I think what you need to tell Owen is that he should get into more trouble. Sometimes that takes away our worries more than being perfect all the time."

Owen scowls down at him and I just laugh and wave, making my way back to the house with Millie by my side.

"Gordon seems to be good for him," Millie says, opening the door for me and helping me get inside.

"He definitely is good for Owen. I've seen more smiles, well, almost smiles from the guy than I did in the hospital or the boutique."

Millie raises an eyebrow. "He's kinda cute, don't you think?"

My insides react in the affirmative, but I shake my head. "I hadn't noticed. I'm sure the grumpiness is a total vibe some ladies go for."

Shaking her head, Millie says, "A real grump is not for me, but I think there's something behind the orneriness he holds on to. It wouldn't be hard to figure out." Why she's looking at me like I need to take on this task, I don't want to even ask.

"What do you have planned for tonight?" I ask, wheeling into the kitchen for a glass of water.

"I am applying to some online schools. I can start studying now and get some credits going while I search for jobs."

I grin. "That's awesome, Millie. Are you going to go to school here in town?"

She shrugs. "I'm not sure. I mean, I missed the actual cut-off for enrolling in-person by several months. And I'm not sure if I can afford tuition out here. But, I've got to make some decisions to keep going. Otherwise I'll go stir-crazy."

"I get that. I got my first tailoring job. It's a pair of pants that the man down the street needs hemmed. So I'll take that as a win." I just wish that I could announce this to all the world at a quicker pace. One pair of pants per week won't do much more than buy me groceries for two days.

"That's a start. I have a few things I need to have you fix as well. And did you make that bear I saw on your dresser?"

I grin. "I did, actually. It's a memory bear for my niece. I used several of my mom's shirts to make it."

"You made that? Would you be willing to make me a few? I know my mom would love something like that with her dad's stuff. Just let me know how much I owe you."

I wave her off. "I'm not charging a roommate."

"You can most definitely charge me. I know what it's like when everyone and their hamster want a discount, especially when just starting a business. My dad is a contractor, and all the family comes out of the woodwork, hoping for discounts or free labor. It makes it hard to keep a company going on favors. I have the money and I would have to pay someone else anyway."

Giving her a grateful smile, I lean over and hug her. "Thanks, Millie. You are one of the most caring people I know."

She laughs. "I don't know about that. More like one of the most naive people you know. But I know a thing or two about business. I helped my dad a lot when Beau headed to college. I spent most of my time doing that, so it was almost a relief to switch gears to become a nanny."

"I can imagine that would be hard. Have you heard from anyone back home since you came out here? Outside of your family, of course," I say, grinning.

Millie's face blushes a bright red, nearly matching her hair. "No one who knows that I exist. I don't do well talking to men I crush on. It's a disease."

"But he asked you to prom, right? So he knew you a little."

Millie shakes her head. "There was a kid I liked after high school. We hung out for a few months until I moved here, and it wasn't until the last week that I realized he was cute. By then, there was no talking to him."

"So he's never tried to contact you?"

"Once, but I was with the kids and it was all a tornado."

"That's always so hard. Has he ever left your town?" When she shakes her head, I say, "Well, look at that. All your experience and knowledge from being out here means you definitely exist. And our house wouldn't be the same without you."

"I think you should think about Owen, Evie. I mean, the guy is cute and he has a stable job. That should count for a lot."

We both laugh together. "It's sad that our standards can be so low."

Millie nods. "I know that's generalizing a bit too much, but we have to have the bar set and then all the good qualities only catapult them upward."

"True."

The front door opens, and Kenzie gives us a maniacal laugh. "So I'm cleaning out this warehouse and the lady wants everything gone. You'll never guess what they have there."

"What?" I say, trying to figure out what would make her so happy that we would want.

She pulls out a picture on her phone and all I see is a sea of pink.

"Why are you showing us this?" Millie asks, squinting to see the screen.

"Because we can use it." She pauses as we both wait a moment. "Ready for the next prank?"

18

OWEN

"What happened?" Even pressing my finger next to my ear only helps me hear Gordon's voice a bit better.

"It's...everywhere...no good...Come," is all I can make out.

"I'll be right there." I'm not sure where he is, but I grab my wallet and slip on my shoes. I head out the door and run to catch a cab, dropping someone off next door.

"Will you take me to this address?" I ask, sitting inside and rattling off the address I memorized days ago. I'm a bundle of nerves the entire way there, hoping Gordon didn't slip and fall or anything. He's been cautious ever since he came home from the rehab center, but I don't know if he's got a full adventurous streak where his mind tells his body that they're really only twenty-five again.

It isn't until the car turns the corner that I see what I'm assuming he's talking about. Instead of seeing a somewhat green and brown lawn because of the fall weather, it's a sea of pink with small dots of white and black.

I pay the driver and get out, almost paralyzed by the

number of pink flamingos stuck into the ground. How long did that take and where did they get them all?

"Isn't it amazing? It's probably the best prank yet." Gordon is sitting on the porch and I've never seen him so happy.

"Are you hurt? Did you fall?" I say, giving him a quick up-and-down glance. It doesn't seem like he sustained any injuries.

Gordon shakes his head. "No, I just wanted you to see this. If I could figure out how to get a picture from my phone to yours, I would've sent it."

"That's got to be a thousand dollars' worth of flamingos right there," is all I can say, ambling up the driveway and to the porch. How would Evie have been able to afford this? Not that I think she's bad with money, but she did just quit her job. Could she have already found a job with a significant signing bonus? Anything is possible.

"You might be right about that. My little app here says that nine of these cost about thirty dollars."

There are too many to even count. "I'm surprised you don't have a TV station out front here."

Gordon laughs again. "It wouldn't surprise me if someone called about it. I'd think it would be more along the lines of against the city's ordinances rather than getting positive attention."

Several cars drive by slowly. There are two kids in the back of a car and I can see them with their mouths in an O-shape and their fingers pointing toward the flock of flamingos.

I take a seat next to Gordon on one of the rocking chairs. "So you're okay then? I thought you were going to say you'd fallen and needed help to get up."

"I'll make a note of that for the next time I need you, and fast. You must not live too far away."

Shaking my head, I say, "No, I'm pretty close."

"Did you get dinner?" Gordon asks.

I hesitate, not sure what I'm supposed to answer on that front. My grandmother's offerings were often leftovers that had freezer burn or expired since before I was born.

"I had a late lunch. Do you need me to get you anything?" I ask, leaning forward a moment.

Gordon shakes his head and points to a car pulling into the driveway. A woman steps out of the car with a plastic bag of food, staring at the pink landscape as she brings it toward us.

"Order for Gordon A.?" the woman asks.

"That's me," he says, taking it from her. He extends a folded bill and the woman thanks him and goes back to staring at the pink eyesore before getting back into her car and driving off.

"Look at you learning how to use technology, Gordon," I say, relaxing back into the chair. There isn't a complete absence of noise because we live in the city, but sitting here, relaxing on a cool fall afternoon is something I haven't done in years. I'm usually sleeping until moments before I need to leave for the hospital.

"Who said I didn't know how to use it? How do you think I've been able to buy all the stuff for our pranks?"

I shrug. He just told me he doesn't know how to text a picture, but he can do all that. "That's what I get for assuming, right?"

"Exactly. You can't always take people at face value. They're bound to surprise you."

"Yeah, usually in the wrong way."

Gordon opens the plastic wrapping around his utensils

and then opens the box, revealing pasta. "Was it actually the wrong way? Or you just couldn't see the signs of what was happening until it finally did?"

Man, the guy gets right to the heart of things.

"You have a point there."

"You betcher dollar I've got a point. Sometimes we get so wrapped up in ourselves that we can't take a step back and analyze the situation from another angle. Did your ex-girl-friend communicate with you well?"

I pause to think about that for a few moments, finally shaking my head. "Her toxic trait was the silent treatment. I remember one time asking her why she did that. It would take me days of analyzing every conversation and action I could remember to figure out why she was mad. It could've been solved so much faster if she'd just told me what was wrong rather than expecting me to know her every need."

"And what about your communication skills? Did you tell her everything that was going on with you?"

I nod and then slowly shake my head. "No, not always."

"Why?"

"Because she would've freaked out. Like me even consid-ering a job change or spending my time on a new hobby was wrong somehow. That was a red flag I never saw coming."

"So, you're not blameless either. Which is fine, son. But you remember this for the future. You don't just give up and never try again."

"Ouch. Are you a mind reader or something?" I say, rubbing my forehead as if I'd felt him invading my thoughts.

"No, just an older version of you, son. If I can spare you some of the troubles I went through, I'll feel a lot better about things. These are the kinds of chats I always pictured myself having with a son."

My throat tightens with the emotion coming through. It

takes at least a full minute before I can speak without my voice sounding like a preteen. "I always wondered what it was like to have a talk with a father figure."

"Your dad wasn't in your life?" he asks, waiting for my answer before lifting a swirl of pasta to his mouth.

Shaking my head, I say, "No, he bailed when he found out my mom was pregnant with my younger sister. I was only two at the time, but I can remember snippets of it happening. He hasn't contacted us since I was almost four. Even when my mother passed away last year, I expected to hear something from him, but the phone call never came."

"That's a tough lot, son. But you've made it to this point and I'd say you're fairly successful. Well, everywhere but in the love department."

"Wow, I'm getting burned by an old man," I say, laughing.

"We get older and we don't have time to beat around the bush. Cut right to the point," Gordon says, taking a bite of the piece of bread that came in the meal.

"I'm not giving up on it. I think I just need a couple of weeks to get my head on straight. Figure out what I really want in a relationship."

"What ideas do you have so far?"

"I've definitely put communication on there after your pointed discussion on the topic," I say, laughing.

Gordon chuckles and says, "At least you were listening." He coughs and it sounds deep in his lungs.

"Are you all right?" I ask, leaning closer.

"Just the change in the weather. This happens to me every year."

His dismissal doesn't ease the niggle of worry creeping into my mind now. "Do you have any more check ups scheduled for your leg?" I don't want Gordon to get defensive, but I'd feel better if I could hear what was going on in his chest.

"I'll go in a week or so. Why?"

"I should drop by with my stethoscope tomorrow. I would like to check your lungs."

"I'm an old man. Everything in my body sounds like starting a 1920 Ford. Old and chug-like."

A car pulls into the driveway next door and I watch to see who's in the car. A magnet on the side of the vehicle says something about organizing. The woman walks to the back of the car and pops the trunk, pulling out a scooter. Kenzie.

That's when Evie gets out of the backseat, while a blonde woman exits the passenger seat.

"What do you think?" Evie says, laughing as she points to the flock before us.

"That's pretty impressive," Gordon says. "It will be hard to top five hundred flamingos."

"More like a thousand," Kenzie says. "Some lady bought an old warehouse and they had boxes and boxes of them. I knew just the person to put them to good use."

"The question is what to do with them now." My words are foreign to my own ears.

"Leave it until the snow hits," Evie says, leaning on the half-fence. "That would be fun to see."

The blonde woman shakes her head. "Naw, take them and leave them at random houses and businesses. It would be funny to see what people think."

Gordon nods. "That could be another adventure. I like it."

"As long as the adventure doesn't end up in the house, I'm okay with it," Kenzie says, laughing.

"Boundaries are set," Gordon says. "I need to prepare for

the next challenge." He raises his arm like he's holding a sword and, as funny as it looks, I hope that's how I am when I grow old. Carefree and not afraid to be myself.

A few things I still need to learn.

19

EVIE

I don't think I could've come up with a better prank than the flamingos. I kept three of them in my closet for a rainy day. It was difficult hiding them from Kenzie, though.

Hillary and Kenzie went on a job together earlier today and picked me up from downtown, where I was interviewing to work at a medical office. The two of them had to pick up a few more supplies for some major cleaning adventure and headed out right after. To be honest, I'm surprised Hillary went willingly.

Gordon goes inside his house with the help of Owen. I'm sitting on my own porch when a notification pops up. I'm supposed to meet with an orthopedic surgeon today. In thirty minutes, to be exact.

I'm a little sweaty from all the exertion done on my scooter today, but I might as well call a car and head out soon. Maybe he'll be able to tell me I can walk on the boot and get rid of the scooter. It's not the ideal situation, but anything is better than constantly tripping over rocks and cracks.

I'm waiting on the sidewalk and see Owen walk out, waving goodbye to Gordon. He sees me and actually waves. Did something happen to him in Gordon's home? Or is this a prank of his own?

"Hey," I say, wondering if I should just ask him why he's not pretending I don't exist or leave it in a peaceful silence.

"Are you going somewhere?" he asks. He strolls over with his hands in the pockets of his shorts and I'm stuck in a vortex of checking him out. The guy is strong and so very attractive. And his face isn't screwed up with a frown, which means I can really study him. Powerful jaw, a hint of a dimple on one side. The way his slightly curly hair has all the bounce in the world. He probably wakes up like this.

I'm so lost in thought, I almost forgot he asked a question. "Um, yeah. I'm heading to the hospital. I've got a meeting with the orthopedic surgeon there."

"Which one?"

"Which hospital? Or which surgeon?" He sits down on the grass next to me and I need to break whatever focus I have on this guy.

"Surgeon. I assume you'll go to Boston Health, right?"

I nod. "Yeah, but I can't remember the name of the surgeon. I figured I'd just go and ask at the desk who they have me scheduled for."

"Probably a sound plan. Do you need help?" he asks, looking up at me.

"I'm waiting for an Uber. From there, I'll wheel myself into the hospital and hopefully find a working elevator."

He frowns and says, "Do you have bad luck with elevators?"

"Just once, when I was working for a corporate lawyer in high school. We were on the twelfth floor and the elevator was broken for the entire summer I worked there. I guess there was a dispute between the owner of the building and the company for who should've had to fix it, and so they drew it out. So anytime I need an elevator, I cross my fingers and hope it works."

Owen chuckles, and I can't help but stare. "I can see how you'd be worried about that with a scooter. Do you need help? I can help you if you need. I forgot something in my locker the last time I worked, and I could definitely use it again before my next shift."

"Um, sure. Yeah, that would be great." Am I going to survive a car ride with this guy? He's been nothing but ornery to me since we've met and yet, I can see the rays of a unique personality shining through every once in a while.

Should that mean anything to me? Probably not. Chances are high that it would just turn out to be one-sided if I start to like him. Which I'm not.

No way.

The car pulls up and he opens the door and helps me into the car and then takes the scooter to the trunk.

When he gets into the car, I turn and look at him. "Sorry, why are you doing this? Don't you have things you need to do?"

He gives me a small smile. "I left the key to my mailbox in my locker at work and I was going to find time to go get it today anyway."

I narrow my gaze at him, as if that will cause him to exclaim he was just joking about the whole thing. But why pretend to need to go to the hospital just for me?

We go through the entire drive just talking about the weather and the forecast. I might as well journey back to the land of nineteenth-century Britain at this point.

Once we get to the hospital, Owen gets the scooter out of the trunk and then opens the door and helps me out.

"I don't know who taught you manners, but they did a great job," I say quietly. I have to get the compliment out, but I don't want him to think I'm hitting on him.

"Thanks, it was my mom."

"I appreciate it. I thought my older brother, Drew, was the only one to do something like that these days." Swallowing hard, I realize how awkward I'm making this. "Okay, so the surgeon. Let's go."

We get into the elevator and press the button corresponding to the map on the wall for the area. To be honest, I just let Owen guide me.

We stop on the next floor up and Owen stiffens as soon as the door opens. He steps closer to me, almost as if I can protect him from something outside.

"Are you okay?" I ask in a whisper, since he's right there anyway.

All I see is a quick shrug of his shoulders as his gaze stays forward. A woman walks in with a few others, dressed in scrubs and her brown hair back in a short ponytail.

"Owen," the woman says, her eyes wide. "What brings you to the hospital this early in the day?"

"I'm helping Evie to the surgeon's office."

The woman leans over to look around him at me. She says nothing before standing back up. "Another one of your dates?"

I don't know why I bristle at the woman's tone, but I can tell there's some history here. Her question also makes me wonder what type of woman he goes for.

"What do you mean, another date?" Owen says, staring at the ceiling of the elevator.

"Denise went into depth about your date last week. In the cafeteria. Are you trying to get me back, Owen?"

Okay, ex-girlfriend in the flesh. This is getting interesting.

My thoughts take me back to the night I was in the ER with Kenzie, and she said something about me looking like Owen's ex. From the quick glimpse, I don't see it.

"No. I can date whoever I want, just like you did while I was gone. If Evie and I want to go on a date, then we will, all right?"

I reach out to touch his arm, hoping it will help him calm down. The doors open and I'm just grateful for more space and some genuine air out there instead of the stuffiness inside the elevator.

"Good luck," the woman says as she walks off in front of us.

Owen turns to me and runs his hand through his hair, making it stick up all over. "Sorry about that. Um, that's my ex-girlfriend, Riley. I, uh, didn't realize she was working right now." He turns to see that Riley is walking toward a large sign that labels the surgeons on call.

"I'm going to run and get that thing from my locker. Call me when you're done with your appointment. I'll make sure you get home. Okay?" He grabs a paper from a nearby desk and jots something, handing it to me.

His phone number.

He's long gone before I have the mental coherence to move. I've never had a guy give me their phone number like this. Sure, there was the obligatory exchange when we were getting things set up for events in college, but that was usually me instigating the exchange. I didn't even ask for this and I'm still confused how I feel about it.

It's a practical decision. He helped me get here and he's willing to help me get back home. It would be weird having to page the entire hospital for a nurse who's not even on shift.

By the time I get to the surgeon check-in desk, I'm trying to stop the loop of Owen pushing his phone number into my hand that's happening in my brain. This is why I've never been more than a friend to any guy. I'm shocked by the smallest things.

"Evelyn Evans," I say once I see the receptionist.

She nods and checks me in. I have to wait for some time before I'm called back by, you guessed it, ex-girlfriend Riley.

This is going to go over well.

"What happened to your foot?" she asks with a small smile as I wheel in behind her.

"I broke it playing pickle ball," I say, grateful she can't see my face. It's a dead giveaway that I'm lying.

She stops in front of a door and I almost run into her, veering to the left at the last second. "Let's go in here. The doctor will need an MRI to see how things are progressing, and then we'll get you to see him."

I'm taken into the room and I have to sit still while pictures are taken of my bones, this time with the Used-to-Be-Grumpy's ex-girlfriend. I thought the energy in that room was tense, but now I get what people mean when they say they could cut the tension with a knife.

"How long have you been seeing Owen?" she asks, before taking the last x-ray.

"Um, we're not see–"

"Were you friends before he left for Guatemala?" she asks, cutting me off.

Shaking my head, I say, "I met him in the ER when I broke my foot. His friends are the husbands and boyfriends of my roommates."

Her expression relaxes somewhat, and she says, "Oh, so you don't have any interest in him. Good."

If someone had asked me a couple days ago, I would've been able to deny everything. And now, I'm feeling protective of the grumpy bear. If I dated someone like the woman in front of me, I'd probably have to detox after breaking up.

"If you're his ex, why do you care?"

Riley shrugs. "I invested a lot of time into the guy. There are still some feelings there."

I frown. No wonder I don't have a chance with guys like Owen. Their past has a death grip on them.

I wheel into the room where Riley directs me and then sit down on the table. Might as well do that now while I don't have eyes watching my every awkward move. Just as the door closes, I see Riley next to a doctor and they lock lips. There might even be some spit exchanged. I shudder and wonder what her deal is.

Then again, I wonder what Owen saw in her for however long they were dating.

Several minutes later, the doctor that comes into the room is the one who was kissing Riley. That's not weird.

"Let's look at your scans, Ms. Evans," the doctor says. At least he's professional and to the point in the office. He shows me the computer screen with the MRI results. "Okay, from what I see from your first x-rays, it looks like things are healing nicely."

My spirits lift for the first time since I met Riley. "So I can be done with the scooter?"

He shakes his head. "I recommend another two to three weeks on the scooter, at least. You might be able to avoid surgery if things keep healing how they should. I'll tell the receptionist to schedule you for a follow-up appointment around then. Then you might just get to walk in the boot at that point."

"That's too bad. I guess I need a few more adventures with the tricycle."

The doctor gives me a small smile and nods before saying, "Good luck. Have a great day."

I can do this. A couple more weeks of diligence on the scooter will hopefully mean I don't need surgery.

Now I just need to find Owen and go home.

20

OWEN

The coward strikes again. I can't believe I left Evie to go into that office with my ex while I tried to stay as far away as possible. Sure, I could've sucked it up and powered through, but this is the first time I've seen Riley since the breakup. And it didn't go as smoothly as I would've liked.

I wait in the small area near the elevators, hoping to catch Evie on her way out and help her home. She comes out to the desk and gets a card. The scooter is still there, but she's smiling at the receptionist. Even in a less than stellar situation, she's smiling. I might've thought she resembled Riley when I first met her, but I couldn't be more wrong.

"Are you okay?" I ask. My hands are in the way, so I stick them into the pockets of my shorts, which I seem to do a lot in front of Evie.

"Scooter for another two to three weeks, but maybe I should learn how to do tricks. I heard there is a cool skate park near my house." She laughs and says, "And did you know your ex is dating the surgeon? Or maybe they're just kissing buddies?"

I frown and grit my teeth. Figures Riley would go for someone with a higher status. I should've seen this coming at least eighteen months ago.

The doors open and I recognize Riley in the distance. On impulse, I lean over and touch my lips to Evie's. I expected there to be a feeling like she was my sister or something, but all the nerves in my lips are on fire right now. I pull back for a second and go in for a second kiss when she reaches up and touches my face in a soft stroke, blocking out everything that's going on around us.

Is this what kissing is like? I mean, I've kissed a few women, but there's something about this that's different. Maybe that my whole body feels electrically charged all of a sudden? Did I ever feel this with Riley?

No, the woman was always trying to be over the top with everything. But this kiss with Evie is simple and sweet, making my brain hazy as to the consequences of it.

"You forgot this, Ms. Evans," Riley says, causing us to pull apart.

Evie and I look at each other in surprise before she seems to snap out of the reverie and turns to look at Riley. My ex is holding out Evie's phone.

"Thanks," Evie says.

"So much for not dating." Riley glares at me before she walks away.

Evie and I get into an empty elevator, which has to be a miracle from the universe, because that never happens.

"I am so, so sorry for doing that," I say, searching her face for any emotions I can pick out. She's mostly stunned.

"You're fine. I figured you were trying to impress your ex, so I just went along with it." She's so nonchalant about the whole thing, and I'm over here thinking that the kiss was the best one I've ever had.

I turn to face the doors of the elevator. "So, are we okay? You won't be weird around me or think I'm some creep, right?"

Evie laughs and shakes her head. "To be honest, after I saw her kissing my surgeon, I tried to picture a good way for you to get revenge on her. A kiss wasn't what I pictured, but I think it did its job."

I don't know if it's because the kiss was a kind of icebreaker, but it is significantly easier to talk with her about more than the weather on the Uber ride home.

"So, that's your ex-girlfriend, huh?" Evie says with a short laugh.

Leaning forward, I bury my face in my hands for a few seconds. I sit back up and nod. "Sadly, yes. Did I miss a few red flags? Yes, yes I did."

Evie nods like she gets it. "It happens to the best of us. If it's any consolation, I'd pick you over the doctor every time."

I don't know why that warms my chest, but I can't hold back the smile. "Why do you say that?"

"Well, Grumpy Nurse," she says, letting out another laugh, "I think you're not really that grumpy. You're so kind to Gordon and you must have some super sneak power, because I didn't even hear you outside hiding those clues to the treasure hunt."

Ducking my head for a moment, I say, "Thanks. I don't know if many women would agree with you. Being a male nurse rarely holds the clout a doctor does."

"Then they are missing out on a great opportunity," she says.

We stop at her house just after her comment and I'm feeling way more comfortable than I have in the past. Evie looks similar to Riley, but that's about where the commonalities end.

I help her to the door, and my gaze flicks down to her lips, wondering if we could recreate the sparks from the hospital. But her casual dismissal of the event has me taking a step off the porch toward the waiting driver.

What if she didn't think the kiss was good?

"Okay, well, I hope you get some rest," I say.

"You too. Thanks for helping me, Owen. I guess I'll see you during the next prank?" She grins and I nod, wondering what Gordon will have planned for the next event.

"I'll be there." I turn around and get into the car, not looking at the house until I've closed the door. It almost feels like I'm just dropping her off after a date. To the hospital.

There are so many emotions coursing through me it's hard to distinguish one from the other. Being around Evie makes me want to do and be so much. Hearing her compliment me has given me a boost, and I'm ready to search for fun pranks just to make her smile.

And that kiss. I never felt that with Riley.

But am I now relegated to the friend-zone?

21

EVIE

There are only so many words coming to mind for the events of today. I can picture it better as one of those giant swings where they strap you in with industrial Velcro and pull you to mountain heights and then drop you. The initial drop is terrifying, but it's the back-swing that makes the fear increase.

"How did the doctor go?" Millie asks, looking up from a laptop set on the kitchen table.

"Um, doctor?" It's only then that I realize I've been so focused on the memory of Owen's kiss that it's clouded all other rational thought. "Not great. I'm stuck on this scooter for another two to three weeks."

Millie frowns. "I'm sorry. I know you were hoping to be done with it."

I wheel over, my brain still abuzz with all things tall, male, and Owen.

"If I tell you something, will you not tell anyone else? Like not even a peep to your brother or Spencer?"

Millie nods and closes her laptop. She folds her hands and lays them on the table in front of her. "I feel like I should have some guesses as to what you're going to tell me, but I've got nothing."

Leaning in, I whisper, "Owen kissed me."

"What?" Millie nearly shouts. My hand shoots up to cover her mouth and I motion with my finger to my lips.

I give her the quick run-down, hoping she'll keep this secret a bit longer.

"So, you told him it wasn't a big deal? You're making it a big deal."

"I didn't want him to feel obligated to anything if I said I enjoyed it."

Millie frowns. "What if he thinks you're not interested now?"

I hadn't thought of that. "Let's be honest, I don't know what's going to happen. But I know we had a great conversation in the car. Like, there is a real person behind the grump."

"What about HuskyHiker?" Millie asks, drumming her fingers along the table. I feel like I'm taking a test with that sound, and I reach over to get her to stop.

"What about him?" I ask, trying to follow her thinking.

"I'm just thinking that it might be nice to meet him and see where things are going there. Then if things take off with Owen or HuskyHiker, at least you'll know which way to go."

Shaking my head, I say, "I don't think I'm ready for either situation to happen, Millikins." We both grin.

"I didn't say you have to declare undying feelings for either one. I'm just saying that sometimes an informed decision is easier once you've done the research before needing to vote."

With a laugh, I say, "You must be studying something about the voting process."

Millie frowns and nods at the computer screen. "Yep. To

say that I'm glad you came in when you did is an under-statement."

"Now that I've taken at least thirty minutes of your study time, I should probably go take a shower and relax."

"Oh, a guy down the street came by with an armful of clothes for you to fix and tailor. He says you already did a pair of his pants?" Millie asks, pointing to the small room just off the front door.

I wheel over to see the mass of clothing. "That is an armful?"

"Well, it was more like three armfuls from what looked like a kid's wagon."

Again, I'm laughing at how deadpan Millie is about the whole situation. "You're pretty exceptional, you know that?"

"You're basing this assessment off a pile of clothes?" she asks, scrunching her nose as if trying to fit those pieces together.

Shaking my head, I say, "No, just that you see more of the picture than most. Thanks for chatting with me."

"Remember what I said," she says. "You might as well test out the waters to see how it goes."

"I'll think about it," I say. My gut tells me she's right while my brain tells me to stay as far away as possible.

22

EVIE

Have I made a decision about meeting HuskyHiker? No, no I haven't.

Have I had plenty of time to do so? Yep. An "armful" of mending later and I still haven't been able to talk myself into doing it. Which means I haven't even written HuskyHiker for two days out of fear that I might "accidentally" write something I don't want to commit to yet.

I severely underestimated the role of tailoring in the world. The hardest part is figuring out what to charge for all the fixes. That's when my older brother comes into play. He spent an hour on the phone last night helping me come up with prices for certain fixes and even helped walk me through a basic website. We've never been super close before, but the gratitude is strong as I think of Luke right now.

I haven't been given jobs for the memory bears or for wedding gown fixes, but I'm using my talents to keep things going.

"Evie!" I hear at what feels like the crack of dawn

Monday morning. I'd gone to bed late after fixing a formal dress for a woman who has to leave early this morning for a flight and needs to take it with her. I check the clock and realize that I slept through my alarm to wake up to meet her.

I change as quickly as I can with the blasted boot still on my foot. A maxi skirt and a stylish sweatshirt will have to look as professional as I'm going to get in this short of time.

By the time I make it to the door, I see Hillary standing there, staring out at something.

I have to duck under her arm to see out. Rows and rows of clear plastic cups line the dying grass, the sidewalk, as well as the porch. A car is in the driveway and I can see the woman holding out her camera to take a picture of the scene.

"How am I going to get out of the house?" Hillary asks.

"Back door?" I say, wondering how far back the cups go. From the look of it, the woman drove in and smashed a bunch of them, making the driveway a darker color of cement with the water spilled.

"It goes all the way around. How long did this take to set up?"

Hours, at least. I hadn't heard a thing, even when I stayed up late. I'll have to start calling him Sneaky Owen. Stealthy Owen? I'll have to think about that.

"Can I get my dress?" the woman in the car asks when she finally steps out of the vehicle. "I've got to make my flight."

I nod and wheel back to the hook next to the stairs. At least I didn't have to clamber up the stairs to get the dress from where I worked on it.

Making my way back to the door, I hand the dress to Hillary and give her a pleading expression. "Will you give this to her?"

"You're going to owe me. Can't you make up some rules for this prank war that it can only affect you?"

"Sorry, Hillary. I didn't think they'd take it to this level."

She chuckles. "After the sea of flamingos, there's no way they couldn't do something insane like this."

She takes a step down, trying to step in the small space between the cups. Instead, she smashes one on the side and ends up tipping over several in the process, making it look a lot like bowling.

Hillary gives me a glare before kicking several more cups on her way down the porch steps.

"Thank you," the woman calls out. "I've just sent the payment through an app. Let me know if you don't get it. I've got to run now, though."

She practically throws the dress I worked to steam the night before into the backseat and pulls out of the driveway, nearly hitting a car. At least I'm not driving right now.

For some reason, I want to talk to someone about this whole adventure. HuskyHiker is a great candidate. Owen and I aren't at the stage where I can text him about everything, although I could say something about the cups of water. Maybe I'll wait until later.

Our conversations, the ones I have with HuskyHiker, have gone back to a sort of normal tone since he asked to meet, although I still have in my mind the fact that we will probably have to meet in person at some point. What if he's disappointed when he finally meets me?

Me: I don't know if you're online right now, but I thought I'd IM you through here before sending an email.

I wheel myself back to my room to get ready for the day when the phone pings. I grab it but it's just a text for a sale on journals from a company I've never actually ordered from. The products I liked have been stuck in the cart for months. Well, I haven't actually checked that since the day I was thinking about buying them.

Maybe it's better to just write out everything all at once to HuskyHiker521 and send it. Then I won't get distracted and not say everything I need to say.

To: HuskyHiker521

From: The WeddingPlanner2

Here are some of the many questions I always seem to think of after I've already sent you things. So in the interest of not being seen as a stalker or a weirdo, I wrote down a list. Answer what you want:

1. *How did you come up with the HuskyHiker name? I'm guessing because you like hiking, but I feel like there's a deeper story there.*
2. *What are your thoughts on sushi? My roommates think I'm crazy because I can't stand it. Just cook all the fish.*
3. *Have you ever started a business?*
4. *Are you planning to live where you are for life? Or are you planning some kind of hobbit-like journey when you get older?*

That last question makes me think of Gordon. I wonder if after he's healed he'd want to be like Bilbo Baggins and venture out into the world. Then again, Bilbo was very hesitant to do anything outside his comfort zone. Gordon, on the other hand, seems to be gearing up for bigger adventures.

Is this a very random set of questions? Yes, yes it is. But those could start several very in-depth conversations. While we did all the surface-level chatting at the beginning of our relationship, I'm getting to where I want to know more about him regarding deeper topics and opinions.

Maybe it was spurred on by Owen's detailed account of his breakup with his girlfriend, but you can learn a lot about people when they give you more facts. And I can usually tell if someone is lying or being painfully truthful.

Knowing the backstory of a person's username could be significant. Sushi preference? That lets me know if a person is picky or not. Business, because I can use any help to get my tailoring work to at least tide me over until I figure out something else. Or get hired.

Was it a mistake to tell HuskyHiker I wasn't ready to meet?

I stew over that for a few moments as I put on my mascara. No, I think that's what I needed to do. Even now, I'm not quite ready for any big changes in our email relationship. But maybe soon.

My thoughts then turn to Owen. The guy definitely has a soft spot for Gordon. There's no doubt that he was the one filling cups and placing them outside our house in the middle of the night. I'm surprised he was able to do it with minimal light. Then again, I could see Gordon sitting in a wheelchair supervising every bit of it.

Did I misjudge Owen?

He has several characteristics that signal he's not a complete grump.

Paying off his sister's wedding dress and taking the time out to help my elderly neighbor. Escorting a random woman to the hospital and putting up with seeing his ex-girlfriend. That one he got a kiss out of though, so that might have been a benefit.

One swoony, fantastic kiss.

I wish he'd done it because he wanted to and not because Riley was walking toward us.

But then our conversation in the car on the way home was great too. There are glimmers of his personality each time we connect, along with a growing attraction on my end.

So what did I do to offend him initially? All I did was fracture a bone in my foot and then help his sister find the dress of her dreams. Most people would applaud me for doing both back-to-back. Owen just looked at me like he was waiting for a plague. He's probably seen some things in the ER, but I don't know if I need to hit him upside the head or spend more time with him to get him to like me.

Was the other day a fluke? Maybe the more animated Owen will resume his grumpy state just like Cinderella's carriage turned back into a pumpkin.

Ugh, why do I feel the need to get people to like me?

Maybe it's because he's friends with my roommates' men? It's not like we've even hung out as one enormous group, so I don't need to worry about that.

I try to shake it off. There are so many things I bring to the table. If he goes back to being the grumpy dwarf, I'll let him. I won't try to change for him or expect him to change for me.

I've made that mistake before. His name is Todd. I tried to be everything he wanted and it didn't end happily ever after. More like it was a pain that is now a thorn prick every time I think about it.

I'll just take a step back and do my thing. Let the rest of the group handle the falling in love part of life.

23

OWEN

By the time I'm off from my shift on Tuesday, both my phone battery and my social one are depleted.

Somehow, the whole hospital has been buzzing about my supposed new girlfriend. When I try to get details from some of the other nurses, they don't have any names of who started the rumors, but it's not hard to figure that out.

Either Riley spread the lies after seeing how kissing should be done, or Denise caught wind of the whole thing and sent it out to her gossip chain. To be honest, I'm leaning heavier onto the latter option because losing does not look good on Riley.

I sleep at least seven hours in silence and wake up on my own, which is pleasant, especially since Jack and Spencer keep checking on me. Miles sends me texts a couple times a week, and I get a "hey" from Trey at the beginning of the week because of all his training and game schedule.

They don't need to do it, but I'm grateful they do.

Once I turn on my phone, I see I missed a call from Darcy. I call her back and hear, "Hey Owen, I wanted to let you know that we've had to push the wedding back by four days. It's going to be on New Year's Eve."

I try to hear anything in her voice and there's a tinge of anger there. "What happened?"

"My future mother-in-law pretended to be me and called to cancel the venue. She wants us to get married in their backyard. In December."

"Um, is she building a large shed to house everyone in the bridal party?" I say, trying to lighten the mood. It's been a while since I've played this role.

"Not on your life. We had to make an arrangement with the venue to not accept a phone call as terms of cancellation and then pick the first opening they had. At least it wasn't another six months from now."

That's true. "Okay, well, I'll put that in my nonexistent calendar."

"Don't say I didn't tell you," she says before hanging up.

I log in to check my messages from TheWeddingPlanner2 but my mind is momentarily occupied by thoughts of Evie. She was so easy to talk to and there was a serious connection there. But I feel the same with my pen pal.

I smile as I read through the message she sent.

To: TheWeddingPlanner2

From: HuskyHiker521

These are some great questions. Let me take a crack at them.

1. *HuskyHiker started because I love hiking. Husky came because I put hiker into one of those generator websites and HuskyHiker was one of the options. 521 is my birthday, May 21st.*
2. *No to sushi. I can picture it still moving if it's not cooked.*

3. *I'm no help in the business starting department. But I can outsource that to some great people.*
4. *I'm open to moving somewhere different. We've talked a lot about traveling and I would love to do that more. I don't know if I'd put roots down in many places. It would depend on who I meet and the circumstances.*

I try to come up with some questions to ask, but part of me would just like to meet her and see if we connect in real life like we do on the interweb.

What is the top place you want to visit?

I'm still trying to narrow down where I want to take a trip to, but TheWeddingPlanner2 has definitely broadened my horizons and added at least a dozen destinations.

Maybe she'll be the one I can travel with.

24

EVIE

I'm prepping my next prank the following day despite my exhaustion. Hillary called for a house meeting late last night saying that we needed to get the cups of water picked up and soon, because she's had to change her socks a few times since the prank was set.

So I got up early with a garbage bag and maneuvered around the yard on my scooter, emptying the water cups and chucking them into the bag. I lost count around five hundred cups and eventually started an audiobook so I could feel somewhat more productive. We're bound to have the greenest grass this fall.

Now I'm sitting on the upstairs floor cutting shapes into toilet paper rolls. Yes, I know it sounds absurd, but it's a low-budget prank. Put a glow stick inside and it will look like there are critters in the yard.

The internet doesn't always have the best ideas. Okay, so maybe there are too many ideas and mostly ones on the mean spectrum when it comes to pranks.

The phone rings and my dad's name pops up on the

screen. I have to blow out a breath and prepare myself mentally for his calls.

"Evelyn, we're going to have to cancel the Evans' trip to the lake house."

"Okay," I say, confused. We got together in the middle of the summer at the lake house, and I hadn't heard about another event happening there until Christmas.

"Luke and I have to go to Europe to fix some problems in the company. Drew and Tiffany are busy. I just wanted to let you know."

I nod and say, "Thanks, Dad. Is anyone else going?"

Maybe a getaway would be good for me. Thinking about my roommates, it might be good for them too.

"Not that I know of. Do you want to use it?" His tone is clipped, as though he didn't budget in the extra time to talk to me this morning.

"Yeah, I think I need a little time at the lake house before the weather changes. I'll swing by and get the keys tomorrow if that works."

He grunts. "I'll drop them by your house. We're flying out this afternoon."

The fact that he offered to bring me something makes me wonder what's going on. Anything that doesn't directly benefit him usually has to be done by someone else.

"Perfect. I'll be home all day."

"What are you doing next weekend?" I ask the girls in the house when we sit down for the first roommate brunch we've been able to have in at least a month.

"I haven't thought that far in advance," Hillary says, finishing up a text on her phone.

"What's up?" Millie asks. She's been buried in school-work the past couple of days, and I've barely seen her out of her room for more than food.

"My family has a lake house in Connecticut that's open next weekend. I was thinking we could take some time and go as a group. What do you think?"

There's silence around the table for several moments before Hillary says, "Of course I want to go to a lake house. Is that even a question?" The rest of us laugh before she says, "Your dad won't be there though, right? I mean, from our family history, I don't want to cause any drama."

Hillary was set to marry my cousin but ran out before the ceremony took place. It was there that I met Rachelle, and then I moved into the house and met the rest of the roomies. It was an unpleasant situation that turned out for the best. I don't think my dad would see it that way, though. He still holds a grudge, even though my cousin is happily married to someone who stuck around for the vows.

"No, he and Luke are flying to Europe today. They'll drop off the keys later. It's amazing that all of us are here together during the day."

Kenzie rubs her forehead. "I needed some time off after all the jobs I've taken on in the last month. It's great to have your own business, but I'm not very good at managing time and telling myself to take a break."

"That's definitely the truth," I say, laughing.

Hillary nods and says, "I'm not scheduled for any princess parties after this weekend. I'll block out my calendar for our lake house trip."

It's Millie who asks, "Are we inviting the guys?"

There is a chorus of yeses and noes coming from both Kenzie and Hillary. Then they stop and turn to me as if I am the fount of all knowledge. I shrug.

"I hadn't gotten that far."

"I mean, it's your lake house," Hillary says. "You should be the one to decide who comes. But if you need a nudge, I'm team no guys."

Kenzie shoots her a frown. "And if you were magically dating someone?"

Hillary frowns and takes a bite of her yogurt. "I'd probably want him to be invited as well," she says reluctantly. And they are back to staring at me for the answers.

"Why not? We'll have to divide up the food. There are four wheelers and other lake vehicles, but it might be too cold to use any of them."

"Thanks, Evie," Millie says. "It will be fun to get away."

We chat about other things and then Kenzie and Hillary head off to their rooms to get ready for the day. Millie is tapping her fingers along the table as if she's trying to figure something out.

"Is there something on your mind?" I ask. I stand and take the napkin I used to hold my bagel and throw it in the garbage.

"It's kind of a long shot," Millie says, "but I was thinking, what if you decide to meet HuskyHiker521? What if you guys hit it off and end up dating? You could even invite him to the cabin."

I turn to search Millie's face, wondering if she's losing it. "Invite him to the cabin? Why?"

Millie gives me a small smile. "Why not? Isn't it fun to hang out in a secluded spot with all of your best friends and their guys? I mean, you wouldn't feel like the third wheel if you had a special someone coming."

"What about you? Are you deciding whether to bring someone to the lake house? Does Millie have her eye on someone?" We chuckle and she shakes her head.

"That would be a no, unless you count the books I'll be bringing. Does the lake house have Wi-Fi?"

I nod. "Yeah, my dad would die if he didn't have an internet connection. And you're not bringing school books to the lake house. It will be a time to relax and have fun while we're gone."

"I guess I can prepare for that. But I still think you should meet up with HuskyHiker before we go. Then you'll know."

Millie stands and disappears up the stairs, leaving me wondering what to do.

Is meeting my pen pal supposed to be like ripping off a band-aid? Just do it and get it over with? If so, I've been waiting for nothing.

I wash the dishes and tidy up the kitchen, all the while debating what to do about Millie's "advice." I finally pull out my phone and tap in a quick message.

To: HuskyHiker521
From: TheWeddingPlanner2

Do you still want to meet?

25

OWEN

It was only one line and yet I'm sitting here stunned that TheWeddingPlanner2 wants to meet in person. I'm not sure whether to be nervous about the actual meeting or if she'll be disappointed to meet me.

After hanging out with Gordon the past few weeks, I've realized I have a lot more to offer a potential girlfriend than I previously thought. And if I ever get into another relationship, I won't be trying to impress her by bending every character trait I have to make her like me. There's got to be some woman willing to put up with the quirkiness of Owen Young.

I'm thinking about this the whole time I'm working on the next prank set up for Gordon. We saved some of the flamingos in the backyard shed for him and then took several to decorate houses and parks close enough to walk to. I've taken Gordon out on adventures in his wheelchair so he can see them.

The cups of water prank was something I came up with after checking out Gordon's stockpile of paper goods. And the whole prank was epic, even if it took nearly three hours to set up in the dead of night. But I can't deny the happiness that emanates from Gordon every time he sees the next part of the adventure.

So this setup is all on me. I came up with the idea to use walkie talkies to send random sounds throughout the night. Sure, it's not as chill as some of the other pranks, and it will probably freak out the girls, but I almost want to stay at Gordon's overnight so I can see their reaction.

"Of course you can stay," Gordon says. "Then we can laugh about it together."

Every time I'm with Gordon, it makes me wonder if this is what it's like to have a father in my life. Or maybe he's like a grandfather. My mom's father passed away before I was born, so I've never really known anyone but my grandma, who died a few years ago.

"Okay, I like this plan."

I have to make sure the women are all gone before I take an extendable ladder and lean it up against the side of the house. I attach a speaker there, just out of sight as if looking from the inside, and hurry back to Gordon's house.

We order food to be delivered and wait for the gals to get home.

"I feel like we're waiting for a movie to start," I say, laughing as I pop some microwave popcorn for a snack.

"Me too," Gordon says.

The sun goes down and there is just enough light to see the outline of their house from the porch.

"Okay, it's showtime." I pull out my phone and make sure I'm connected to the speaker. The first sound I turn on is a dog barking. With the volume turned up, it sounds a lot like a real dog.

Gordon and I are sitting just out of view under his

covered porch, but I can see someone look out the upstairs window and then disappear.

"What noise is next?" he asks.

"I think we'll go for 'rustling trees'." I press the button and pause to listen as the sounds of scraping branches echo off the side of the house.

"What are you using?" Gordon asks, pointing to my phone.

"Just a bunch of sounds I saved to my phone."

He smiles and says, "Why don't we do the screaming one next? As fun as this is, I'm fading fast and ready for my bed."

I press the sound he suggested and we wait. Not more than a few seconds later, the doors open and out run Millie and Hillary. A few moments later, Evie appears with her scooter.

"What was it?" Hillary asks.

"I don't know. It stopped. Did someone get hurt?" It sounds like Evie's voice.

"We'll have to look around. Maybe she got hurt on the road or something?"

A laugh comes from next to me and I turn to see only Gordon's teeth in the fading light.

"That was fun," he says loudly.

The women turn in our direction, and I know we're caught.

"Gordon? Owen? Was that you?" Evie calls.

"Yeah, it was us," I say, walking off the porch and over to the fence.

She scoots closer and there's a strange glow around her face, as if the moonlight is highlighting all her features. All I can think about is the kiss we shared. And then I wonder if it's bad to be excited to see Evie when TheWeddingPlanner2 wants to meet. What happens if things take off with my pen pal?

"You scared the daylights out of us," she says, balling up her fist and punching me in the shoulder. "I thought a woman had been attacked and we were going to be next."

"Then why did you come outside?" I ask, gauging her reaction.

"Because we didn't think it through," Hillary says.

"Did you hide a walkie-talkie or something?" Evie asks, trying to see through the dim light.

"A bluetooth speaker. Then I just played the songs on my phone."

Evie lets out a laugh. "Songs? Those were not songs. I'm assuming the dog was you too?"

I nod and the other two women turn to go back inside. "And the rustling trees."

"That's what that was. I didn't think we had anything close enough to scrape on the windows, but it's been a long day."

"How's your foot?" I ask, eager to prolong the conversation.

"Still attached," she says. I can't see her face now, but I can picture her smiling as she says it.

"As a nurse, I'd say that's a good thing."

"Thank you for your professional opinion. I've got to get back to work inside, so can we stop with the eerie sounds?"

Instead of answering, I click open my phone and press another sound. "As you wish," which is the sound of Cary Elwes from *The Princess Bride*. I didn't think I'd actually be using it, but this is the perfect opportunity.

She laughs and nearly snorts. "Sorry. That was pure comedic timing right there. Good night, Gordon," she says as she wheels away.

"No good night Owen?" I ask, more to see what her response will be.

"Good night, not ornery Owen."

I can't help but laugh about that. "Touché. I definitely haven't been the most upbeat guy in the past few weeks."

Her laughter lingers even after she enters her house.

"She seems like a good catch," Gordon says with a knowing smile.

I shake my head. "I think I need to start on the friends spectrum before I consider anything past that."

Although I don't think I'll be able to get the picture of Evie's face in the moonlight out of my mind for the rest of the night. Or stop myself from dreaming of kissing her again.

26

EVIE

What was I thinking, asking to meet this guy? My palms are sweaty and my body is so over rolling over all the bumps in the cobblestone sidewalks ever since I made it downtown. A car can only make it so far where we're meeting—Faneuil Hall.

It's a building that has a long line of shops and foods. I figured that meeting in a very public place would be the best idea, just in case I get any serial killer vibes coming from him. Not that I know what those are, but I've watched enough seasons of Law & Order I should be okay. At least I hope.

I got here later than I wanted to since I had to finish mending a large hole a guy had torn in the crotch of his suit pants. But I'm here and I'm ready to get this part over with. Maybe we can part as amicable friends. I don't want to think about what could happen if I'm actually attracted to him. With my luck, it rarely goes both ways. But a girl can hope.

A reminder of our meetup pops up on my phone.

This is it. It's happening. I get that nervous sensation of

birds taking flight in my stomach as I think about why I'm here.

The hall is crowded with people on their lunch break and I take a moment to scan for HuskyHiker.

He told me he'd be wearing an army green shirt that says, "I like big hikes and I cannot lie." At least I know where the starting point for our conversation should go. Because throughout all our conversations, I don't get the vibe that he's into specialty T-shirts.

I think I see someone matching that description and it turns out to be a man with a mullet. Luckily, his shirt has no words on the front, so I'm good there.

I wheel forward a few inches and wait as the throng of people keeps stopping. Through the small space between two people in front of me, I can see army green. While I'm waiting here, I might as well get out the rose pen and classic book I'd told him I would have. Then I won't have to fumble in front of him as well as try to stay upright while on my scooter.

Do I hug him? Is that something I should do? He's pretty tall, if it's him.

Then the guy turns and I see none other than Owen Freaking Young. My gaze drops to his t-shirt, where it says in big bubble letters, "I Like Big Hikes and I Cannot Lie."

I don't know whether to feel relief or sheer terror or excitement that I've been talking to Grumpy Nurse for the past few months.

The mob moves forward as people decide what they want to eat and I tuck the book and the rose pen into my bag. Coward move, yes. But I might need to investigate this situation first.

What if HuskyHiker is just a friend of Owen's and he

asked him to wear it? HuskyHiker could be in the shadows just waiting to judge the form of TheWeddingPlanner2.

I keep wheeling forward, the suspense in my chest pressing down on my lungs and making it hard to breathe.

And then it's like everyone is gone and I'm there in the middle. There's nowhere to hide now. So I pretend to be evaluating lunch options by looking up at the enormous signs.

"Evie?" Owen says, and I turn, flashing him what I hope is a convincing smile.

"Hey Owen. What are you doing here? This is quite the trip to make for lunch." I bite my lip, wondering if I'm signaling too much about why I'm here too.

He frowns and nods. "Yeah, I took a cab. I'm supposed to meet a good friend for lunch."

A good friend, huh? That's positive.

My brain is still spinning with him here, being the guy from my online messages and my in-person favorite kiss of all time. It's hard to put all the things I've categorized as being Husky-Hiker and have them line up with what I know about Owen.

Sure, Owen has been slowly getting less grumpy, but the depth of our conversations and the memories we've gone over are from someone who's strong and has gone through a lot. After meeting Riley and knowing his mother died last year, those definitely fit.

"What are you up to? Touring Boston on your scooter?" There's a hint of a smile at the corners of his mouth, and I'm surprised by how the attraction flare lights up within me. Again.

"Me?" I say, pressing my hand into my chest just below my neck as I try to come up with some reason I'm here other than the actual truth. "I'm supposed to meet someone as well. For work." The last two words lurch from my throat with way too much velocity and volume.

"Did you get a new job then?" he asks, staring at me with his light brown eyes, and I'm having a hard time focusing on much else.

I nod and say, "Kind of. I started tailoring and mending for people. It's not much, but it's paying the bills until I figure out what to do with my life."

He nods and gives a closed-lip smile. "That's always a good idea. Well, I'm trying to decide if I should wait here longer for my friend or get something to eat for my trouble." He raises his wrist to glance at the watch there.

"Um, what time were you supposed to meet?" I ask, trying to keep the casual act going.

"Fifteen minutes ago."

"Is your friend typically late?" I'm the worst.

Owen shakes his head and says, "I'm not sure. This was supposed to be our first meeting."

"Oh," I say with forced surprise. "An online friend? Tinder? Or one of those matchmaking apps?"

He swallows as if the thought of either of those is beyond him. "It's not like that. We've been writing like pen pals for a couple months."

"That's cool. I've always thought pen pals were a fun way to connect with people."

"What do you think? Should I wait or just chalk it up to a misunderstanding?" Owen looks uncomfortable as he sweeps his gaze across the crowded building.

I swallow, feeling the guilt well up in my throat. He might not be heartbroken, but he's definitely feeling something.

"Has she messaged you or anything?" I ask, trying to help even though I'm probably just making things worse.

He pulls out his phone and starts swiping. "Nothing."

"Maybe she doesn't have service. Could she be in a tunnel on the way here? Or maybe she was in an accident and can't message?" I cringe. There's no need to make him think something terrible happened to his pen pal when she's standing right in front of him.

He nods. "Maybe I'll wait another five minutes."

"Sounds good. Could I grab you some food while you wait?" I ask, gesturing to the lines of food.

He glances down the aisle as if trying to figure out what to get and then looks back at me. "What are you planning to get?"

"I thought I'd try a few different options. The Greek place looks delicious, and then maybe something from the Indian place and the breadsticks from the pizza shop. It's a splurge, but I like to try new things."

"You're going to get in line for all those?" he asks, looking shocked.

I shrug. "Yeah, why not? I mean, that way I can try a bunch of things in the same meal. And I can use whatever I don't eat for leftovers."

"What if you don't like any of them?" he asks, and I have to smile at his bewilderment.

I smile and say, "I usually get at least one thing I know I'll like. Then it's not a total waste."

His posture changes as he thinks this over, his shoulders straightening somewhat. He glances toward the doors once more and then says, "Might as well eat."

"Such an eloquent speech."

It's only then I see a smile that reveals his teeth. "I try."

The guy is hot. That sounds like such a crass term when I'm used to everything in terms of Mr. Darcy and the older actors I love to watch through movies, but that's all my brain comes up with right now.

And now I'm wondering why we waited so long to meet. Although he doesn't know everything I know.

We've shared a good chunk of our history through emails and one amazing kiss in person. He's as fully invested in the prank war now as I am. All signs go to green lights and flags to move ahead, and yet I'm nervous. I've been hurt before and it took a long time to heal. What happens if I get hurt and still have to see him every time my friends get together?

27

OWEN

Being stood up is never easy, but I have mixed feelings about it right now. I mean, sure, I was hoping to meet TheWeddingPlanner2 and connect with all the things we've been talking about, but maybe it's too soon. Did I push her into it and now she's backing out and ghosting me?

I hope she doesn't stop messaging me. She's been one half of my lifeline these past weeks.

On the other hand, I'm surprised to run into Evie. Especially this far into the city from where she lives. Getting around without a broken foot is hard enough, let alone using a scooter. At least it's not crutches.

"Okay, so if I want to try some of whatever you're getting, where do we start?"

Evie smiles, nodding. "I'll get a gyro and some souvlaki sticks here at the Greek place and you can go stand in line there," she says, pointing toward a food place two stalls down, which looks to be named something with curry. "Get two kinds you think would be good. Then we'll meet for drinks and desserts after we get this."

By the time I get back to her with a chicken tikka masala and a butter chicken plate, she's managed to hang a bag of food on her scooter handle as we head down to the next spot.

"Do you always do this? Get food from different businesses?"

She lets out a deep breath. "Not always, but when there are options, it's hard to choose, you know? I mean, I am very grateful to have traveled a lot in my childhood, so there are some things I dream about eating or experiencing again. Coming to a place like this kind of satisfies that, especially since I'm now on a severe budget."

I laugh at that. "Sounds like my bank account while going through nursing school."

The drinks are done and I reach out to grab them but have to shift part of the food to the other arm.

"I think we need to find somewhere to sit down, don't you?" Evie says. "I mean, if you want to sit with me. I don't want to force you."

Shaking my head, I say, "I'm actually looking forward to trying out all of this." Evie laughs again and we steer our way over to the small tables in the building. We get everything set out before us and it looks like a ton of food.

"Where do we start?" I say, almost overwhelmed by the choices. Everything smells great.

"Wherever you want. Take a little of whatever you want to try."

My gaze scans the table. "It all looks delicious."

"Then I've done my job as your food tour guide," Evie says with a smile. She takes a forkful of rice in front of us and I do the same.

We're quiet for a few moments before she breaks the

silence. "So tell me about your pen pal. How did you connect?"

My cheeks turn red as my brain goes back to the beginning. "She found me on a forum in a matchmaking app. But we were both avoiding being matched, and then we talked about traveling."

"Do you travel a lot?" she asks.

"No, but I hope to someday."

Evie shakes her head. "You need to. There is a lot to see in the world. And the food is usually good. Minus a few odd things."

"This feels like a first date."

We both laugh. "That is so true," Evie says. "Maybe it's the first date of our friendship."

"You don't think hanging out in the ER counts?"

"No, you were over in the corner being ornery. Then again, I'm sure working nights are rough, so I should give you the benefit of the doubt. But you escorting me to the hospital was a good first friendship date." She frowns and then it disappears quickly.

I nod. "Thank you. Riley broke up with me a couple of weeks before I met you in the ER. I've been volunteering a lot at the senior rehab center too, so that's tiring. It's where I met Gordon."

Her face lights up at the mention of the older man. "He's awesome, isn't he? And while I keep telling myself this prank war is for him, I think it's been good for me too. My dad always said I could be overly serious about things, wanting them to be perfect. When figuring out a prank, it definitely doesn't have to be lined up and perfect."

"I don't know. What you did with those flamingos was pretty close to perfection."

Evie wipes around her mouth with a napkin and says,

"I'm glad Kenzie thought of me when she found them in the warehouse."

"You should've kept them and tried to sell them online. I'm sure people would go for bundles of them."

She frowns. "Now you say something. I could've funded a trip to see real flamingos in Fiji or something." Her lips turn upward and it reminds me of our kiss.

"That sounds like a real vacation."

Evie takes another bite and we fall back into a comfortable silence. I don't think I ever had one of those with Riley. She always had something to say about everything, even the smallest crumb of gossip.

"So, I have to ask about the T-shirt. Is there a story behind it?"

I glance down and laugh, closing my eyes for a second. "I was trying to figure out something distinct I could wear to a first meeting and I figured this would be better than scrubs."

"I don't know. Maybe your pen pal has a thing for a stable career."

For some reason, her comments make my insides spin like those gymnasts on the pommel horse.

"I doubt that. My sister gave it to me. Hiking has always been something I do to release the tension that comes with a fast-moving career. I work nights for a few days in a row and then have time to explore some of the beautiful trails around New England."

"Do you prefer to hike alone? Or do you go with the guys?"

It's been a while since I've done anything with the guys. My last time was brunch when I told them all about the breakup. "I go alone a lot, but I should probably let more people into my life."

"That sounds more like a fortune cookie than how you really feel."

I laugh at that, surprised that my stomach actually hurts from the amount of laughter I've done at this one accidental lunch.

"I guess it's just like this meal. I would've never thought to go to different booths and get various options to try. Sometimes it's easy to stay with what I know rather than branch out."

"I get that. It's the fear of the unknown. Like quitting your job and not knowing what to do next." She goes cross-eyed for a few seconds and then laughs.

"What are your plans? Do you want to go back to working at a wedding dress place?" That sounds awkward, but my brain blanks on a better phrase.

She doesn't say anything for several moments, her gaze focused on the small piece of dessert in front of her. "I loved the overall job. Finding a dress for someone who's tried on dozens of dresses before and finding the one that makes her say, 'That's the one!' is the best feeling in the world. But there's no way I'd go back to working with Judy."

"She seemed like she had a few quirks."

Nodding, Evie looks like she's trying to decide what to say. "The hardest part was that she didn't take into consideration my ideas. I was all in. I wanted the business to thrive, but there was a lot that just didn't go the way I thought it should in a professional setting. Like when she had me go fix the dress and left your sister waiting forever. How is Darcy, by the way?"

"Good. Working on getting everything planned for the wedding. She likes to get things done early. It was a surprise that finding the dress took her a while, but I think it's because she wanted Mom to be there."

My phone pings and I see Gordon's name on the text.

Gordon: I've got the perfect prank. When you're done with work, we should plan.

I laugh, shaking my head. "Gordon says he has ideas for another prank."

Evie grins. "The guy is always thinking. Do you think I've unlocked an unhealthy obsession inside him?"

"No. I don't know too much, but he was in hospice last spring. If anything, having something to look forward to is a good thing."

I glance at the time on my phone. "Oh, dang! I've got to get back. I'm covering for a coworker. Thanks again for introducing me to all this food. I'm not good at picking out things on my own."

"Any time," Evie says. "Good luck. I'm sure I'll see you around Gordon's later."

"True. Let me take the garbage."

"Oh, I don't know if you have to work or not, but we're heading up to a lake house in Connecticut next weekend. The roommates voted to bring along all the guys. So if you haven't gotten an invite, here it is."

I smile, liking the idea of a weekend getaway. "Thanks. That's good to know. I haven't been the best at keeping up on the group text lately. You might've just saved me from Jack breaking into my house while I'm sleeping again."

Evie bursts out laughing and says, "Why can I picture that in all its awkward form?"

"Because the guy is consistent." I throw away the nearly empty plates and wait as she gets the leftovers packed back on her scooter. We walk out into the fall weather and I take a deep breath. There's something nice about the crispness of it.

"Okay, I've got to head out. Are you good?"

She gives me a quick nod and says, "I've got this. Good luck today."

I head out to catch the train. While the day didn't turn out how I thought it would, I felt like I made progress with Evie. The only thing that could've made it better is moving out of the friend zone. As much as I want to meet my pen pal, Evie is real and considerate.

And unlike Riley, she doesn't have to talk over me or control the situation.

Everything I see from Evie makes me wonder why I stayed with Riley for so long.

28

EVIE

The next week is busy as I juggle the few mending jobs I have with searching for another, more full-time gig. And on top of it, I've got to come up with a flexible itinerary for the cabin.

I've always been taught to be a delightful host, especially when it's to some property the Evans family owns, and that education is kicking into high gear. Menus, activities, other activities that those with a bum foot can handle, etc.

The thing I keep coming back to the most is that Husky-Hiker521 is Owen Young. I wonder if the t-shirt is where he got the screenname. I know he says it was from a generator but Big Hikes could also translate to Husky Hikes.

Owen is tall and broad, but I don't think of him as husky. Then again, he probably put that in there to ward off anyone hoping to hookup or wanting a long-term relationship.

Our lunch was off-the-charts good. Comfortable, fun, and actual laughter coming from Sir Grumpiness. It goes to show that my bar for men in the past has been very skewed, probably because I thought my brother Drew was the ultimate last unicorn when it comes to guys like that.

And now, I think the prickly exterior on Owen is more of a defense mechanism. His bright smile at the end of our lunch is now imprinted on my brain.

I've seen him over at Gordon's as they planned what turned out to be Tootsie Roll pieces spread out on the grass to look like dog poop and then again after we used the knock off version of Post-It notes to cover the entire front of Gordon's house. There are some visible spots where pieces fell off, but it's what works with the small budget I have. There's no way I could've finished that without Hillary and Millie's help.

It's hard to not think about everything we've talked about online and not have it add to the attraction growing inside me when I think of him. But he's been adamant that his pen pal is just a friend, so that's probably the best I have to hope for.

By the time I've packed all the food and snacks along with my own suitcase, I know it's going to be a tight fit in the SUV Drew dropped off for me early Saturday morning. I'll be taking at least seven of us, but the reality is, with all our stuff, it is going to be more like four or five people can cram in the back.

A few of the guys show up about fifteen minutes after we said to meet, but Hillary isn't packed yet, so we're still waiting.

"Thanks for inviting us, Evie," Trey says, holding Kenzie's hand. And now I'm jealous of a hand. Not because I want to hold Trey's appendage, but because I'm picturing Owen's broad hands and wishing I had some kind of connection going on, too. Maybe it was a bad idea to invite him.

"No problem. I haven't been out of the city since our mud run adventure a few months ago, and that doesn't count as a vacation."

"Agreed," Jack says, leaning against what looks like his vet truck.

I glanced around, trying to figure out how many people we have. "Okay, we need to figure out rides."

"We're riding with Dani and Miles," Kenzie says.

"What, are the couples sticking together now? It's so hard to be out here in the single world," Jack says, dropping his head in mock sadness.

Spencer rolls his eyes. "You want them in the backseat making out?"

Jack makes a face and says, "Good point. Good luck, married couples."

"Okay, Jack, how many can you take in your truck?" I ask.

"Two. With the way Spencer packs, he's already filled up most of the back seat."

I nod and point at Spencer and Beau. "You two with Jack. Keep him on his toes now. No betting until we get to the lake house."

The guys laugh and give each other high fives. Hillary finally comes out with two suitcases in tow. "You know we're coming home Sunday night, right?" I say, chuckling.

"Yes. But I couldn't decide what to leave, so I brought it all. At least I'll be prepared."

"That's a great way to look at it," I say. My eyes search the group for Owen, but he hasn't shown up yet. "Okay, so all the single ladies will be in the Suburban then. Or we can take some of the stuff in your truck, Jack, and then you can add someone else. Or I have room in here for everyone."

"We'll take Millie," Spencer says, smiling at my room-mate. She blushes and nods, walking toward the truck.

"Well, at least it will be the two of us," Hillary says. "We can have a single gal catchup session."

"Do you have that much to tell me about your life?" I ask with a laugh.

Hillary shrugs. "I mean, we can go back as far as life in the third grade, but that would be reaching. And the details might be fuzzy."

"Don't let her kid you," Jack says. "She's got the memory of an elephant. Telling you everything in detail is her specialty."

Hillary frowns at Jack and heads around the Suburban to the passenger seat.

I point to where Jack can add the two bags he's holding onto. He stuffs it into the small space and heads back to the truck.

"Okay, is that everything?" I ask, trying not to make it obvious that I'm looking for Owen. Maybe I freaked him out at lunch the other day?

"I'm here," says a deep voice, and I try to hide my smile when I see Owen come from Gordon's house. "Sorry, he needed some help with a few things."

Owen sees the trunk of the Suburban and looks confused what he's supposed to do with his bag. "We can put it in the backseat. We don't have too many people riding with us, so we've got the room," I say.

We get his bag into the back and I say, "Is Gordon going to be okay for the weekend?"

Owen nods. "Yeah, I asked my sister to check in on him. The guy doesn't have any family still alive and I'd hate to come back and find he's injured himself."

Be still my beating heart.

"Am I in the Suburban? Or should I go with Jack?" Owen asks, turning to look at the truck.

"We're full here," Jack says, leaning out his window. "But I'm glad you came. It's been a while, man."

I point to the SUV and say, "Just hop in here. We've got Hillary."

Owen opens the door behind me to get in. Hillary opens the passenger door and says, "How about you come help navigate, Owen? I'm the worst at keeping focused."

"Doesn't Evie know how to get there?" Owen says, glancing over at me.

I'm frozen, unsure what to say or do. "It's been a while, but I can manage the GPS."

Hillary gets out and sits in the second row, essentially laying down with a blanket over her.

"What about a seat belt?" I say, wishing she wouldn't be so awkward right now.

She's pretending to snore, and I give Owen an apologetic glance before getting behind the wheel. Owen walks around and takes the passenger seat. If he can tell this is a weird set-up, he doesn't let on. If Millie spilled the beans to Hillary about my connections with Owen, we're going to have some words once we reach the lake house.

After stopping at the gas station and filling up all the vehicles with both gas and snacks, we set out on our trip.

"So, this place we're going to, do you go there often?" Owen asks. Hillary is actually asleep this time and I'm tempted to slam on the brakes hard enough to throw her off the seat.

"I grew up going there a lot. It was my grandfather's lake house and now my dad and his sisters share it. They get certain weeks out of the year up there."

Owen nods. "That's cool. Miles has a house we've been to a few times. Definitely a lot of memories made there."

"I can imagine they have a cool spot. We have a cabin

near where Hillary and my cousin were supposed to get married a couple of years ago."

He coughs and says, "Wait, what? Hillary was married?"

"Kind of. Almost. It was a weird day. She ran away right before the ceremony. I started renting from Rachelle in the house we're in now and Hillary came back a couple of months ago."

"That makes sense," Owen says, running a hand through his hair. "Jack always talked about a Hillary. From all the bickering they've done, I'm putting all the pieces together that she's the one he knows."

As if in answer to that, Hillary lets out a long snore, causing Owen and me to laugh.

"How's your week been?" I ask, not wanting there to be too much silence.

"Good, just working and pranking you. What about you?" He turns his gaze on me and I'm grateful I'm driving to have to look away. I'm pretty sure he can see my thoughts written across my face.

Letting out a long breath, I say, "Just getting things ready for this weekend. And researching new jobs. I haven't gotten much traction on my memory bears and I'm not sure how to get in touch with brides who want to add something to their dress."

"What do you mean?"

"I saw this cute idea where a bride took her mother's wedding dress and used a few pieces to add to her gown and then had the rest turned into a robe to wear while getting ready."

"You could do that?" Owen asks, looking surprised.

"Sewing is kind of my superpower." That gets both of us laughing. Everything about this moment feels amazing.

Thank you, Hillary, for giving me this chance to talk to Owen even more.

He nods. "I'll have to tell Darcy about that. I think she said something about adding pieces of our mother's dress to her day. That would be the perfect solution." He pauses for a moment and says, "How's your foot doing?"

I shift my left foot over a bit, as if testing it before giving its status. "Good. I've been able to put a little weight on it when I need to, but for the most part, I'm sticking to the scooter."

"That's probably for the best." He shifts a little in his seat and says, "What plans do we have for the weekend?" He yawns when he says it and I can see how tired he is.

"That's up to each person who's there. I've got a bunch of activities we can do as a group or people can divide up and go their own way if that's what they want to do. But this is supposed to be relaxing, so if you just want to hang out and watch movies or nap the whole time, that's totally fine."

He smiles at me and I have to turn and look at the road as my heart does the uneven bars. I'm not supposed to fall for anyone right now, when I don't have a job and when I'm pretty sure I'll be in the friend zone for the rest of my life. It's a curse I no longer want.

Positivity. I'm never going to get anything when I'm thinking like a Debbie Downer.

Owen kissed me, even though it was to show up his ex. And there was a flicker of surprise on his face after we broke apart. There's definitely a chance.

There's another yawn from the passenger seat and I laugh. "Take a nap, Owen. I'll get us there in about three hours."

"Are you sure? I feel bad making you drive while we all sleep." He glances back at Hillary and then over at me.

Waving it off, I say, "I'm the host, so don't worry about it. I'll just continue listening to my audiobook."

He settles in and closes his eyes. Man, the guy is freaking gorgeous when he doesn't have a constant scowl on his face.

I cue up the audiobook and start listening, trying to remember where I last listened and what happened before.

"Can you really understand this?" Owen asks, opening one eye.

Nodding, I say, "Yep. I like the speed to be at two or two and a quarter speed."

"How can you understand anything that's going on?" he asks. I reach over and pause the audiobook, and he says, "Sorry, I didn't mean to interrupt."

"You're good," I say. "I can concentrate when it's that fast, but if I have a conversation, I miss a lot of the plot and have to rewind."

"Have you always been able to listen that fast?"

"I think I just built it up to this point. There are some narrators who make it hard to understand and I'll slow it down, but for the most part, this is the sweet spot."

Owen nods and looks as if he's deciding whether he should go back to sleep. "What genre is this book?"

"Urban fantasy. I love mysteries and solving them."

"Are you a true crime junkie?" he asks.

Shaking my head, I say, "I can't get into a lot of the crime podcasts. The idea that those things happened to real people and aren't just made up is kind of hard. I do enjoy Law & Order though."

He smiles. "I didn't take you for a mystery fan."

"What did you take me for?" I ask, laughing. It's mostly nerves.

"I don't know. I guess more of the romance type because of selling wedding dresses."

With a wave, I say, "I go through times when I love a good romance, but I usually end up feeling like I've missed out on something by the end. Fantasies and mysteries focus on things other than the heart."

"Unless that's the cause of the death," Owen says, smirking.

I laugh, nodding. "True. What about you? What are your favorite books?"

He looks like he's just been asked to take a pop quiz about something he's never studied. "Um, I don't read."

"What?" I'm pretty sure my heart stops with his confession.

"Okay, I should rephrase that. I've read nothing but scientific journals in a couple of years. Nothing really stands out to me as being worth the time to read it."

"I might just pull over and kick you out, Owen," I say.

He chuckles and says, "It's not that I'm opposed to reading. I think I need some more suggestions."

"I've got a few I can help you with."

We spend the rest of the drive talking about our likes and dislikes in books, and I've even gotten him to download a couple of apps for reading or listening to audiobooks.

I turn on the audiobook after explaining several of the previous plot points and then just start it over from the beginning. While this seems super nerdy, there's something about this entire experience that is exhilarating.

I just wonder if I should tell him that I'm his pen pal on this trip.

But would that change what I feel is a budding relationship right now?

29

OWEN

I can't remember the last time I went on a trip outside of school or work obligations. With my mother being sick for a long time, I wasn't able to go anywhere too far and usually did just for the day, making sure I was home to check on her at night, unless Darcy was around to take a turn.

It took a while to get ready for this trip. Packing and then arranging for Darcy to check on Gordon, before going over and helping him get a few things ready for the two days I'd be gone. At least Evie had given me a heads-up about it because Spencer didn't call me until late last night and I was so groggy from being asleep that I didn't register much.

A few weeks ago, I was irritated that Evie looked so much like Riley that I might've taken my feelings out on her a bit. But talking to her over lunch the other day and then again during the car ride has been almost healing for my soul.

But then there's the twist. I'd been attached to my pen pal, almost thinking that something would develop from there since we'd been able to communicate so well. Is it bad that I'm starting to catch feelings for Evie?

Evie is a person who has opinions, but she's also considerate, kind, and supportive. She spent the time walking me through how to use my seldomly used library card on my phone so I could check out some books. Now I might have another distraction besides just hiking. Or something to listen to while I'm exploring.

We pull into a large white house and the lake is right in the back of it. Usually people I know who have a "lake house" say that when they're a couple miles away from the actual body of water. I only have to take a few steps around the side of the house before I see a sizable dock out back.

"Wow, this is incredible," I say, shaking my head. I turn to see Spencer, Jack, Beau, and Millie all wide-eyed and still as statues.

"You grew up here?" Millie asks.

Evie gives a soft chuckle and says, "Just for various holidays. My father is a workaholic and we didn't get away as much as I would've liked, unless he was taking us abroad. But this is a pretty great place to make some memories. Let's go unload, and I'll show you all to your rooms."

The inside of the house is almost as amazing as the outside view. Everything is done in whites and pale grays, with a few sections of black as accents.

"My dad hired an interior decorator to redo the house once my grandfather passed. I remember the old wood paneling and shag carpet," Evie says, her eyes glassy as if she's picturing it.

"This whole place is a vibe," Hillary says, glancing around.

"Just think, you could've come up here often had you

actually gone through with your wedding," Jack says to Hillary, his tone somewhat bitter.

I'm not sure what's going on between those two, but it's best if I stay out of it. Spencer is chatting with Millie and ends up hauling her bag upstairs to her room. Is there something going on between the two of them? Maybe I've just been so wrapped up in my own work and misery that I've missed most of this.

Evie sets down a paper on the main kitchen island and says, "Here is a list of activities you can do over the next two days. I'll get dinner started tonight and we'll eat in about an hour. Sound good?"

The group splits apart, some of them heading back outside, while others go unpack.

Evie busies herself in the kitchen, pulling out several plastic containers of cut vegetables and what looks like raw meat. She puts them all on skewers, alternating the vegetables and chicken. By the time she's done with one, it's a colorful kebab.

"Do you want some help?" I ask, sliding onto a stool at the bar.

She glances up and gives me a small smile. "You should head out and enjoy the scenery. There's a hike just a quarter mile down on the right. It'll take you around the lake."

As much as that sounds like something fun to do, I'm more drawn to sticking around here. "I'll try that out in the morning. Let me help you get these going."

Evie thinks it over and then pushes all the containers over before walking around to sit on the stool next to me. "Grab different veggies and add them to the stick. I'll just grab a sheet pan to put them on for the grill. I think we're going to need quite a few."

"This looks amazing."

She blushes and says, "Thanks. It took some time getting it ready this morning, but I figured we'd all be tired and ready to eat when we got here. I've also got a couple salads and some fruit to go with it. I just hope it's enough."

"If it's not, I have a feeling the stockpile of snacks Jack and Spencer packed will be fine." I jut my thumb toward the front door where I had just seen them walking toward the house with armfuls of boxes and bags.

Evie laughs when Jack appears with a bag hanging from around his forehead. "You look like you're stocking up for winter."

"We can eat a lot," Spencer says. "Where would you like the snack section to be?"

With a quick movement, Evie slips off the stool and works her scooter around the island to a pantry door. "In here will be perfect. Go ahead and organize it how you want."

"It better be nice," Kenzie says, walking in with an armful of blankets.

"I'm still waiting for you to organize my apartment," Jack calls out as he walks into what is a really spacious pantry.

We get through several more kebabs when Evie asks me to go out and start the grill. I'm not a master at doing things like that, but I can pretend for now.

Nearly an hour from when we started putting the food together, everything is ready. We've got all the food piled onto a large outdoor patio table that has a few more chairs than the people in our party.

"Thank you for dinner, Evie," Dani says, reaching for another two kebabs, putting one on her plate and giving one to Miles.

"Owen helped me out, too," she says, waving in my direction.

I wipe my mouth with the napkin and shake my head. "It was a learning curve. I'm just glad we have a few people who don't mind charcoal food." I look at Trey and Miles, who didn't even balk at the few blackened kebabs I didn't turn soon enough.

The sun is down and Evie turns on several of the lights that line the deck. With the fading light and the scenery out back, this is the most relaxed I've been in years.

Several friends head to bed as it gets late, claiming they want to get up early to make the most of the morning and the lake house. Evie sits in a long chair, bundled up in a blanket and staring out at the stars.

"Penny for your thoughts," I say on impulse. It was something my mother always said to me. Having said it now, my throat tightens up as a wave of missing her washes over me.

"Isn't it baffling that what we thought was going to be the future turned out so differently?" She doesn't glance over, and I wonder what's got her waxing poetic.

"So we're going for the deeper stuff tonight, huh?" I say, scooting my chair closer.

Spencer, Millie, and Beau are still at the table, chatting about the company the guys are building. The two couples have already gone to bed, or are watching a movie. I lost track.

Evie gives me a smile I can barely see, a lot like that night when we were next to Gordon's fence. "Sometimes it's good to do some introspection, at least to make some sort of outline for the coming months."

"And what are you planning?"

"Twister is definitely off the list," she says, laughing loudly.

Millie raises a hand and says, "Yes! No more Twister."

"What about your past was different than you thought it would be?" I'm not usually one for invading with personal questions, but I find I'm more than curious about Evie's background. She's got to come from some money, seeing as this house is a couple million dollars in value, but she's so down to earth. It's a weird juxtaposition for my brain since Riley came from a humble background but was always putting people down to get what she wanted.

"I'm actually jealous that you're a nurse," she says, giving me a small smile. "I was working on my clinicals at Boston Health and so close to finishing my nursing degree but never finished."

I sit forward, very invested in this story. Although I didn't work the day shift, it was possible I'd seen her before. Then again, I'd been blinded by Riley during all that time and probably wouldn't have given Evie a second glance.

"One morning I woke up unable to see anything. Like completely blind. I went to several doctors to see what could be done, but none of them had an actual answer for it. Most attributed it to my inability to handle stress. So I gave up nursing and started working as a receptionist. From there, I got the job at Bridal Oasis."

"Is that all they thought it was?" I ask, trying to puzzle through several symptoms.

"That was the final conclusion for most of them. My sight came back a few weeks later and because my life was a lot less stressful, I believed them. Do you think it could've been something else?"

I rub my hands over my face, trying to focus on the much-needed details. "My mother had multiple sclerosis. By the time she was diagnosed, the medicine wasn't as effective as if they'd caught it sooner. That last year of her life was tough and I know she had some black out episodes, even moments of blindness." I think through all the criteria to diagnose it. "Do you have trouble with balance or anything like that?"

She points to her foot. "That could be some sign of my abilities here." With a sigh, she says, "I've only ever wanted to make a difference in people's lives. For a while, I felt guilty that I'd failed to become a nurse. And then I'd reasoned that helping women find the right wedding dress was helping, even in a different way."

"Are you kidding? My sister went to five dress shops before. I should say we went, because I had to tag along. You made her feel more comfortable and seen than any of the women in those other stores did. I never saw you as a nurse, but as a wedding dress saleswoman, you won my vote by helping my sister through some of her insecurities."

Evie dips her head and says a quiet, "Thanks."

She stretches her arms over her head and yawns. "I think I'm going to call it a night. See you in the morning?"

I reach out, taking her hand to help her up. A zip of electricity shoots up my arm, reminding me of the live wire I became after our kiss. She's shivering despite the blanket and I realize how cool it's gotten next to the water.

The scenery is picturesque, and if we were alone, I'd be tempted to recreate that kiss.

She disappears inside and I turn to see Jack, Spencer, and Millie all watching me.

"What?" I say, trying to figure out what they might've overheard that would make me embarrassed.

"You two make a cute couple," Jack says.

"We're friends," I say, suddenly wishing that it didn't taste like sand on the tip of my mouth. "We didn't want to hear you drone on about your production costs and overhead."

"Touché," Spencer says.

That breaks up the group and we all filter into the house and to our rooms.

I go over the conversations for the day. Something about our conversation about Hillary's almost wedding triggers a few bells. Would she be using the Love, Austen app and my pen pal?

While that wouldn't be the worst thing in the world, I kind of wish I'd been able to meet my pen pal before we came up here. I'll be spending a lot of time with Evie and I have a feeling anyone else might pale compared to her.

30

EVIE

The boys went for a hike and took some of the fishing poles, leaving the girls to our own pursuits. We drove into town to the cute little Main Street there and walked/scooted through a few of the stores.

Dani, Kenzie, and Hillary were discussing what would be cute to help decorate Miles and Dani's house while Millie hung out near me and my scooter.

"I need a new Christmas ornament," she says. "I love getting them from all the little places I've been. It helps me remember the trip."

"I love that idea. Except most of my travels were when I was much younger and didn't have to worry about the cost to get there."

We laugh a bit and Millie says, "How was your conversation with Owen last night?"

"It was great. It's like he's a totally different person lately. I might have to stop referring to him as Grumpy Nurse in my mind." I actually haven't thought of him like that in quite a few days.

Millie and I laugh as we comb through the thousands of Christmas ornaments.

"I know I've been a zombie studying for my classes, but how did your lunch go with HuskyHiker?"

I glance around the room to make sure no one else is within earshot. "He's Owen."

"What?"

I nod. "I got there and he was wearing the shirt that was supposed to signal it was him."

Millie is practically bouncing up and down. "So? Are you dating now?"

With a frown, I say, "I didn't tell him it was me. I acted like I was just getting some lunch there before meeting someone who needed tailoring."

Millie grasps my shoulders and shakes me gently. "Why? When you're that close, why wouldn't you just tell him?"

"Tell who what?" Hillary asks from behind me, causing me to jump.

"Um, tell my brother to, uh, take his baby in to get a checkup. She wasn't feeling well before we left."

Hillary frowns, as if trying to decide if I'm telling the truth. She finally turns away and I give Millie a look that says she can't be spilling the beans, and especially not this weekend. I don't need a roommate intervention. I've been on the other end of those and I won't take it as well as Kenzie did.

We get back to the house and I collapse in a heap on the couch. A few minutes later, I feel a blanket laid over me as I fade off to sleep.

Who knew keeping secrets and a broken foot could make someone so sleepy?

31

OWEN

This place is incredible. The scenery, the hike, and the lake are all something I needed. There's a spot where the leaves are such a vibrant color I wish Evie was here to see it. She seems to find joy in the smaller things, and I like that about her.

Being here makes me think about Evie more and more, studying her for an extended amount of time. She's so interesting and is the perfect host. When we went to Miles's cabin, it was a free-for-all with food and there wasn't any organization for activities. This trip is so different with Evie taking care of everything.

But then the guilt seeps in that I should wait until I meet my pen pal to have feelings for anyone.

"How's it going?" Spencer asks, walking over and slapping me on the back. We've been sitting in a cove off the lake with fishing lines in the water for the past hour.

"It's going. Nothing is biting." I haven't even had a nibble, but then again, I've never been the best fisherman. I've been too in my mind to care if I catch a fish or not.

"I don't know. I think you might have a bite on the line."

He gives me a big grin and I'm trying to figure out what he's talking about. A quick glance at the water shows I'm in the same lake as a few moments ago.

Shaking my head, I say, "Are you blind? There's nothing on the end of the hook."

Spencer laughs. "Not actually. I'm talking about your love life."

I freeze. There has been no indication of anything happening in that arena. Sure, I've had feelings crop up for Evie and some for my mysterious pen pal, but there's been nothing outward that the guys should've picked up on.

"What do you mean?"

"You've been part of the prank war and you helped Evie last night with dinner, then sat with her out on the porch. Is there anything going on there?"

Okay, some of my friends are a lot more perceptive than I gave them credit for.

"She thinks I'm a grump. We're making our way to friend status."

Spencer laughs. "A grump, huh? I guess she's right about the last few weeks, right? But she just needs to hang on for a bit to see the real Owen."

I frown. "What is the real Owen?"

"Dude, you're the person we can all call for help if we need it. And you have way better manners than either Jack or myself. If it's Evie you like, I applaud you, man. She's heads and tails above Riley."

"Why didn't you say something when I was dating Riley then?" Irritation surges and I reel in the hook.

"We tried to, but you were a little love blind."

Blowing out a breath, I say, "You're supposed to do an intervention or something. Tell me I'm wasting my time if you see something that's off."

Spencer gives me a small smile. "Would you have listened?"

I pause a moment. As I go through my feelings for Riley, I probably would've shrugged their comments off as being jealous that they weren't in a relationship like I was. "What makes Evie different?"

"Well, for one, she doesn't try to pull you away from your friends. She actually brings us all together, like here."

"Riley doesn't have a cabin."

Spencer throws his hands into the air. "Stop being so stubborn. It's not just having a lake house at her disposal. She brings everyone together for things. The flamingo prank? Beau and I were there helping Evie and company to set that all up."

I put the fishing rod down on a rock after connecting the hook to one of the loops on the rod. "You all helped and said nothing? I could've used your help with all the water cups."

Spencer laughs and says, "I'm sure you could've. Look, Owen, I know it's hard to get over a long-term relationship in just a few months, but don't let Evie slip through your fingers because you're still hoping Riley will come back."

"I'm not hoping Riley will change her mind," I say slowly. "When I helped Evie get to the hospital last week, I saw Riley. And at the end of the appointment, I leaned over and kissed Evie as Riley was walking toward us."

I've never seen Spencer so shocked in my life. "You kissed her?" he says in a whisper, glancing over at the other guys down the bank who are all focused on the fishing.

"Yeah."

"How was it?"

I shake my head. "Life altering. But she shrugged it off as being a show for my ex."

"Now what are you going to do?" Spencer asks, shifting

back and forth from one foot to the other as if he's getting ready for a race.

With a shrug, I say, "I don't know. I also have a pen pal I met through the Love, Austen app. So I'm kind of stuck here."

Spencer leans in closer. "Man, how did I miss all this? Have you met your pen pal?"

"No," I say, standing. I need to move while I think about everything. "We set up a meeting, but she didn't show. Evie was there, though, and we had lunch that day."

Spencer claps his hands together and nods. "That's what I'm talking about. That's perfect. You've already made progress here."

"But what about the pen pal? What if things are supposed to work out with her?"

"Well, tell her you need to meet so you can decide some things. If she ghosts you again, go for Evie. Did your pen pal say why she didn't come to lunch?"

"She said she got really sick and had to go to the doctor."

Spencer smiles and says, "That's when you say that you could've helped her with all your nursing skills. CPR with a little kissing action."

I roll my eyes. "She doesn't know I'm a nurse."

Spencer stops moving entirely, staring at me with a dead expression. "Wait, what?"

"We haven't told each other a lot about our personal lives. Only a few things here and there."

"Then why the hangup? You know a heck of a lot more about Evie than your pen pal."

I mull that over for a few seconds. He's right, but there's that connection of the messages from my pen pal helping me get through my breakup.

"I just don't want to be worried about anything, to regret anything, you know?"

"So, what are you going to do this weekend?" Spencer says. "You can't be giving mixed signals to Evie."

He has a point there. My mother would kill me if she knew I hurt someone.

"I'll have to figure it out."

I take my fishing rod and start walking toward the lake house. It's a long enough walk that I have some time to think things through, but I'm not at the introspection part of life.

Breaking up with Riley wasn't something I could control. But the decision to go after Evie or wait to meet my pen pal is something I can ruin, and fast.

32

EVIE

It's almost three o'clock when I finally wake up in the afternoon. The house is abuzz with chatter as all the guys have come back.

I sit up and pat my hair, making sure it isn't sticking out at all angles, as I scan the room for Owen. That's not a good sign. I shouldn't be worrying about him from the first moment I wake up to when I go to sleep. But I had such a wonderful dream about our kiss that it made me feel all the feels.

Hillary and Kenzie are in the kitchen, which is a scary thought. I can't smell anything burning yet. Trey looks like he just got back from a long run and Spencer, Beau, and Jack are all at the kitchen table playing a game.

Dani and Miles are missing, but with them still being in the newbie phase of their marriage, it's not unusual. That leaves Owen missing.

I stand and head over to get a drink of water. My knee aches on the scooter and I'm ready to be done with it.

I leave the group inside and head out to the back porch. The scene is surreal as the trees are all changing colors. But something about the water soothes me, making all my anxieties chill out a bit. Mostly what to do about Owen.

Am I supposed to be the instigator of a relationship? Maybe that's where I've gone wrong before.

"It's pretty, isn't it?" a deep voice says from behind me.

I jump and turn my head to see Owen sitting on a chair in the shade of the house.

"I didn't see you there. Have you been sitting out here the whole time?"

Owen stands and nods, coming over to the railing where I'm standing. "Yeah. I just needed a little solitude."

I grin. "Fishing didn't give you that this morning?"

Laughing, Owen says, "No. Spencer kept talking my ear off." His smile fades as he looks at me for several moments.

"Penny for your thoughts?" I say, remembering him saying that the night before.

He takes a deep breath and lets it out slowly. "I don't know what thoughts to share. They're all kind of jumbled in my brain at the moment."

"Sometimes the best way to figure them out is to say them in the order that they come to mind and then you can unravel them. I have to do that a lot."

"I have a pen pal," he says, his voice trailing off.

"Right, I remember you talking about her at lunch." I try to mask my surprise at him bringing up this topic right now.

He rubs his hand over the back of his neck, his gaze focused on something in the grass below us. "How do you know if someone you know only through paper should or shouldn't be with you?"

It's weird that he's discussing my alter ego with me.

"I think you just need to ask the questions you're trying

to figure out. Did she ever say why she didn't meet you that day?"

"She was sick and had to go to the doctor."

"Talk to her again, maybe set up another meetup. That's the best way to know anything, right? To know if you connect in person." I pause for a moment and say, "Do you want to pursue a relationship with her?"

Owen doesn't say anything for a few moments before he turns his gaze to me. "I don't know," he says, his voice so soft I have to lean in to hear him. That only leads me to a better view of his lips and all the sensations and feelings from our first kiss come back. For a whole five seconds.

It's then I realize that the kiss really was to make Riley jealous. What if he's hoping she's his pen pal?

The clouds of doubt descend, and I'm sent straight back to my life post annulment from Todd. Doubts try to creep in, but I shut them down.

I can't be living in the past if I want something to change in my future.

I give him a wide grin and say, "Go write to her. It's never good to let the questions keep tumbling in your brain like a dryer."

He gives me a quick smile and nods. "I'll have to do that." He looks like he wants to say something, but he closes his mouth and leans forward.

My insides react like a rogue firework and I'm trying to stay chill as he gets closer. It's so hard to wait until the last second to close my eyes, but when I do, I feel nothing.

Then his arms go around me and pull me in for a hug. Well, that's not where I thought this was going.

He lingers, and it makes me think of the "leaning" situation in the movie *While You Were Sleeping*. I might have to rewatch that movie and compare notes. I hug him back, trying to stay focused on why he's hugging me rather than focusing on his physique, which is pretty nice from my point of view. But I'm not supposed to zone in on that.

"Sorry," Owen says, getting all awkward and backpedaling.

"You're good," I say. Lame, lame, lame. I should have the guts to go up and kiss the guy, to be the strong female character with gumption who goes after what she wants. But the fear of being left brokenhearted controls me right now and I can't say anything else.

He gives me the barest of smiles, reminding me of when we first met, but now it's more tender. I feel no irritation at this grumpy man, but an understanding of a small part of what's going on in his brain.

And that's when I know that my feelings for Owen Young have landslided to the edge of a cliff and I'm hanging on by my fingertips.

33

OWEN

I think I just made things worse.

There has to be some magnet on Evie that keeps pulling me toward her. I search her out and want to spend time with her. And then I feel guilty that I'm not giving TheWeddingPlanner2 the chance. But like Spencer said, I know Evie a lot better than I know my pen pal, at least with the deeper stuff.

Kissing her was my original thought when we were out on the deck, but I thought better of it. I don't want to do anything without knowing how she feels first. So I went for the extra-long hug, which might have been as potent as a kiss.

Evie smells like vanilla and cinnamon. It made me think of our lunch together and all the things I'd learned about her. She sounds like she's well-traveled, or at least she was when she was younger. That's always a bonus because Riley wasn't a huge fan.

TheWeddingPlanner2: Do you have time to meet this week?

. . .

I HAVE to pause as I think through all that has happened over the past few weeks. TheWeddingPlanner2 has done an amazing job of keeping me grounded and helping me work through my breakup. But it's the everyday interactions I've had with Evie that draw me in.

Me: Sure. Where and when?

I PANIC A BIT, not sure how to go about that. I'm curious enough to meet up with my pen pal, but my heart is already kind of taken.

I glance up to see Evie in the kitchen, chopping up something. There's something about her expression that makes me curious about what's going to happen next.

She slams the knife down onto the cutting board, takes a ketchup bottle and squeezes it all over before calling out, "Help! Help!"

A few of the guys and gals come running in and Evie holds up her hand with one finger down and covered in red, as if she'd cut off her finger. I stand to see that she's using a piece of carrot as the "lost appendage".

The room erupts as Millie runs over to get a towel while Kenzie and Dani are screaming and can't look. Spencer stays away, which is understandable because he hates the sight of blood, and Jack is the one who gets closer and holds up the carrot.

"Really? You're resorting to pranking us now?" he says, laughing.

Evie grins. "I might be addicted to it."

What was my life like before I met Evie? Definitely not

as fun and adventurous. She makes me want to be a better person and to go for my dreams rather than what society says I should be doing.

"That means I need to move out," Hillary says, rolling her eyes. From what I've heard, she wasn't a fan of the rows of water cups in the yard.

"How did you know it was a prank?" Millie asks Jack.

He turns and points to me. "The first sign was the nurse not reacting to an emergency. And the second was the ketchup bottle sitting on the counter."

Several people laugh, and I watch as Evie laughs and cleans up the mess. There's something special about that woman. She's been through a lot, but she still puts a smile on my face.

We decide to watch a movie half the group hasn't seen and Evie walks over. "Is this seat taken?"

I shake my head and pat for her to sit down. She brings a blanket with her, cuddling up underneath it.

"My pen pal wants to meet," I say, trying to gauge her reaction.

"Really?" she asks, turning to look at me. "Are you going to meet?"

I sigh and nod. "I told her yes, but what happens if she doesn't show up again?"

"Then you'll know where to put her in your life." Evie gives me a quick smile.

"Does that bug you?" I ask.

Evie turns to me and stares into my eyes for several moments. The movie is playing in the background, changing the lights that glow on her face.

"A few weeks ago, it might've irritated me, but you've got to do what makes you happy, Owen. Maybe she's the one you can start a relationship with. But sometimes it's nice to have that closure and know for sure if things were supposed to work out."

"That's true."

"You'll never know until you meet her. Maybe she's a gorgeous model. Or maybe she's got a large hump on her back."

I laugh. "Wait, what? Gordon mentioned the same thing."

Evie laughs too. "There are a host of reasons she might not have met you the first time. She could've been scared of your scowl."

"I didn't have a scowl?" I say, trying to remember my twenty minutes of searching the crowd for my pen pal.

"You were definitely scowling."

Great, that's the last thing I need to hear. Instead of dwelling on that, I lean over and say, "The chopped finger was perfect, by the way."

She beams at me. "Thanks, I was kind of missing our prank escapades."

We settle in to watch the movie and my brain is going a hundred miles an hour. I'm comfortable sitting here watching a movie with Evie. But is her nonchalance about my pen pal a red flag that she's really not that into me?

She hugged me back when we were out on the deck, but she's a fairly touchy gal, so that wouldn't be a total signal of how she feels.

What a mess. Maybe I should go on a hike and come back in a few weeks.

34

EVIE

Breathe, Evie. Just breathe.

I didn't think I'd be this nervous. I mean, it's just Owen. But it's not *just* Owen. The guy has my heart all wrapped up around his finger, and I'm just hoping to make it through this meeting without ruining an already great relationship.

Am I a little bugged it has to come to this? Yeah, but that's my fault for not being upfront with him from the moment I realized he's my pen pal.

"Are you ready for this?" Millie asks. She's experimenting with some necklaces I have on a board on the wall in my room.

"I don't know. It will be nice to be done with this whole charade. I just hope he doesn't hate me for not telling him."

Millie frowns. "Do you think that would happen?"

I lay back on my bed, staring at the ceiling for a few moments. "I hope not, but I guess anything can happen."

"What are you hoping for?"

As much as I've pictured meeting Owen as TheWeddingPlanner2, I usually stop the picture around the time we both see each other.

"I guess we can at least remain friends if he doesn't have feelings for me. The goal is to be blunt and see where I stand. If I'm not someone he can see himself dating long-term, then I'll just cry for a bit, not in his presence, of course, and then keep living my life."

"Of course you would say that. You sound a lot like Hillary right now."

I laugh. "Maybe that's what happens when you live with someone too long."

"What are you using to distinguish yourself from the crowd?" Millie asks.

"I told him I'd be wearing this," I say, pointing to the sweatshirt I'm wearing. It's a graphic design that says, "I closed my book to be here."

Millie laughs and shakes her head. "That will definitely help you stand out. I don't think I've seen that before."

I've got about an hour before I need to leave. But my phone rings and my stomach flips when I see Owen's name on the screen. Why would he be calling right now? Did he already find out that I'm TheWeddingPlanner2?

"Hey, Owen. What's up?"

"Sorry, I don't know if you're busy tonight or not. That Judy lady is claiming my sister's dress isn't paid off. I'll pay for it again if I have to, but I'd rather not give her any more money."

"Slow down," I say as all the words filter through my brain and connect. "Judy is holding the dress still? She usually keeps it until closer to the wedding and does the alterations on it, or has some grunt do it," I say. Like me for all those weeks.

Owen takes a deep breath and says, "Darcy asked to have

some of our mother's wedding dress incorporated into the dress before I told her about your skills. Judy claims that they don't do that. When Darcy asked to take the dress and get it altered somewhere else, Judy refused to give it to her, saying we haven't paid for it."

"Give me a few minutes and I'll drive to Bridal Oasis. I might make it before closing."

"Thank you," Owen says, gratitude in his voice. "I didn't know what else to do and I didn't take the receipt from you when I paid for it."

"No problem. See you in a few."

I'm about to head out of my room when I remember that we're not meeting for the pen pal meetup right now. I grab another sweatshirt and throw it on, tucking the other bookish one under my arm so I can bring it with me.

Is this another ghosting moment? I just need to be strong and tell him how I feel. Hopefully all the chips land where they should.

35

OWEN

I've probably looked at my watch fifty times in the last twenty minutes. Sure, I'd love to meet my pen pal face-to-face, but I can't bear Darcy's tears to go on any more than they already have. She's just a few weeks away from her wedding and there has already been enough drama with her wedding dress as it is.

Darcy has gone through at least a handful of tissues, and I'm pacing the sidewalk outside the bridal shop, searching for Evie to roll up on her scooter. I should've thought about sending her a car or something.

A black SUV pulls up and I realize it's the same one that we took to the lake house.

Evie parks the vehicle with the front sticking out a bit, but hopefully she won't have to stay there long.

I grab her scooter out of the trunk and meet her on the sidewalk.

"Okay, what's the situation? And why does this feel like an old-time standoff?" Evie says with a smile. That gets Darcy to loosen up a bit.

"I'm so glad you're here," Darcy says. "I just want to take

my dress and have someone add a few details from my
mother's dress to it. Owen says you might have the receipt?"

She shakes her head. "I don't have it on me now, but I
can find it fairly quickly. You might have to help me distract
Judy to get to it."

"Let's do this," I say, determined to help my sister and get
to the meetup on time.

We walk into the store and Judy is helping fluff out the
dress of a bride up on the pedestal-thing.

"Welcome—" she says, cutting herself off. "Why are you
here?" She's looking at Evie.

"I just forgot something when I quit." Evie walks over to
the computer at the front of the store.

"You can't touch that," Judy says, stomping over to us.
"You're no longer an employee."

I try to block Judy, but for being such a small woman,
she's strong enough to push me out of the way.

"I need one thing and we'll be out of your hair." Evie
taps away at the keyboard before Judy walks over and pulls
the keyboard away. It's Bluetooth, so at least none of the
wires are ruined.

"You shouldn't be logging into the computer system
here."

Evie turns to her, a determined look that transforms into
intimidation. "Judy, I did everything I could to make sure I
was learning from you and was a model employee. I've got
notes on several times you've cheated both myself and
customers out of money or product. Do you want me to take
legal action on that?"

I try to hide a smile at the way she's showing her
strength. There isn't hesitation there like when she quit.

"You have no proof of anything."

"How about you trying to pin me with the cost of a dress

that can be repaired without ruining the integrity of the dress? Darcy set up a payment plan, but Owen paid it off not even an hour later. The dress is hers, free and clear. If you don't give it to her right now, I will get one of my father's lawyers to make sure you don't sell another wedding dress ever again."

Judy's face is pale white and looks like Evie's words slapped her. "There's still no proof that it was paid in full."

"Give me the keyboard and I'll find it." Judy finally relents, and it takes all of two minutes for Evie to locate my card and the transaction.

Judy's lips pinch together and she storms toward the back room.

Darcy leans in for a hug, her tears returning, but for the good this time. "Thank you so much."

"Don't thank me yet. We need to get the dress before we celebrate," Evie says, grinning at me.

Judy tromps back toward us and hands Darcy a large bag.

"Make sure it's the right gown," Evie says, staring Judy down.

Darcy unzips the bag and confirms it's the correct dress.

"You're not going to take legal action, are you?" Judy asks as we get close to the door.

"Do better, Judy," Evie says before heading outside, her progress slow with the scooter.

The door closes and I fist pump. A surge of adrenaline pours through me at the victory. "That was awesome. Look at you go, Evie. You were on a roll there."

She nods and gives me a small smile. "I realized I need to stand my ground. Especially for friends and family."

I don't know which part of that sentence I want to be more. Friend or family.

Darcy loads the dress into the back of her fiancé's vehicle, and I glance at my watch. I'm going to be late.

"Do you need me to drop you off somewhere?" Evie asks, walking to the trunk to load her scooter.

"If you don't mind. I just need to get down to the harbor." I slide into the passenger seat and we take off. It's dark out now, and all I can see inside the vehicle is the lights highlighting the buttons and the dashboard.

Evie adjusts the volume to the radio and sits back, focused on driving through the Boston streets.

"Thanks for doing that," I say again, trying to figure out a way to cut through the tension. Is there tension? Or am I just imagining it?

"No problem," Evie says, giving me a quick smile.

"Did I interrupt your plans?"

She turns to look at me for a moment and then back at the road. "No. I was just hanging out at the house."

We get to the harbor and she pulls over. There isn't much traffic here this late in the evening.

"Thank you for all you've done," I say, facing Evie.

With a little laugh, she says, "You already said thanks."

"No, I mean for a lot more than just tonight. For cheering me up with pranks and fun when I wanted to be miserable."

Evie grins. "I think we both have Gordon to thank for that."

There's a long pause before I say, "I'm going to meet my pen pal. What do you think?"

She blinks several times but says nothing for a long moment. With a shrug, she says, "Why does it matter what I think?"

I feel like I've just had a bucket of ice water dumped over me. Have I misread this situation completely? From the conversations, to the hug and kiss, to my skyrocketing emotions when she's around, I was convinced she felt something for me.

Blowing out a breath, I say, "Maybe I haven't been the best at showing it, but I like you, Evie. But I get that you just want to be friends." Saying the words is like being punched in the gut with each syllable. "I'll just talk to you some other time. Thanks for the ride."

I get out of the SUV and take several steps toward the cafe. Frustration, anger, and irritation course through me that I read the situation all wrong. It would probably be best to just avoid the opposite sex for the next thirty years.

Reaching out for the doorknob to the café, I hear a sound behind me and turn to look.

"Owen," Evie says, trying to wheel over to me. It's dark out and I can only see her silhouette coming closer.

"It's fine, Evie. I just misread everything and I'll be—" It's then that she comes closer and I see the words I'm supposed to see inside this cafe. "I closed my book to be here."

Evie is TheWeddingPlanner2?

"Are you—"

She nods, swallowing hard. "I can understand it if you're mad that I didn't say something sooner or—"

In the best impulse move of my life, I lean forward and kiss her, sparking the fire that I felt the day I kissed her the first time.

When we break apart, there is a small audience clapping for us leaving the café. Evie's cheeks turn a deep red and she motions for us to go over to the railing next to the harbor. The temperature is low, but I'm nearly sweating right now.

"Are you sure you're okay with this?" Evie says, motioning between me and her.

"Are you serious? This is way better than I was hoping

for. I wanted it to be you. Even more so after that display at the bridal boutique."

"I'm sorry I didn't tell you sooner. I was nervous that you wouldn't want to date me because of...things. Our pasts."

I shake my head, reaching out to tuck a lock of hair behind her ear. "Evie, you've been there for me since my breakup. You've encouraged me and given me the chance to better myself. We both have pasts, but I prefer to think about it as those things preparing us for this moment."

Her gaze drops to my lips and I lean in again, kissing her as my heart bursts.

"So, where do we go from here?" Evie asks.

"Evelyn Evans, will you be my girlfriend?"

She grins. "I'd absolutely love to. As long as you're okay hanging out with a girl with a bum leg for a few more weeks."

"You're worth the wait."

EPILOGUE
EVIE

I wish I had the secret of how to get over the terror that is telling someone you like them. The conversation Millie and I had a few times comes back a lot when I can't believe how lucky I am to be the girlfriend of such an amazing human being.

We've survived a few more pranks from each other, with Gordon's excitement egging us on. Darcy was married in a beautiful ceremony on New Year's Eve, and she looked stunning in the dress I modified with pieces of her mother's wedding dress in. I had enough material to make her a robe out of the rest of it for the actual wedding day. I've worked with several other brides on similar designs and created memory bears for just about everyone who lives in Wyoming. Okay, just the ones related to Millie.

If you're wondering, Owen and I took the time to check the matching app for our compatibility and it was almost off-the-charts. If only we'd been brave earlier, we might've been able to get our relationship started sooner. But then again, we might not have confided in each other as well.

My foot healed well, but other scans showed I have

multiple sclerosis. That was a hard few weeks, as I didn't want Owen to have to go through everything he did with his mother. I gave him the chance to opt out, but he said, "Every minute with you is worth a hundred minutes without you."

The good thing is there are a lot of things to help with it and I'm finding a pain medication that works.

I'm still living life, hiking with my boyfriend and sewing daily. I just finished a job interview with Meg Austen to run the bridal shop attached to their offices. Crossing my fingers I get that one.

By the time I get off the bus, I can see there's already something decorating the front yard of the house.

Flamingos are all over the yard, just not as many as we put on Gordon's lawn. And posters are strung across the trees.

"Owen has an important question for you." By the writing, I'm guessing Millie helped with this adventure.

We've been talking about taking a trip together. Maybe he's come up with a few ideas.

I walk up the sidewalk and glance up at the porch to see Owen standing there in a suit with a bouquet of roses.

And then it dawns on me. Is he going to propose? Movement in the windows signals that my roommates are watching the entire thing.

"Evelyn Evans, Evie," Owen says, grinning at me, "We've been dating for about six months now and I'm pretty sure I can't imagine my life without you. I want to travel the world with you and with our future kids, to laugh and grow old together, through all the good times and bad. Will you marry me?"

I nod, trying to hold back the tears. In the time we've been together, my time with Todd seems like a distant bad dream. There's been healing for both of us.

"Yes, yes I'll marry you!"

He pulls out an Easter egg and opens it to find a few pieces of chocolate candy. "Um, I have a ring, but I think it got switched out with one of the eggs we spread out on the lawn."

I tip my head back and laugh. "If this isn't the perfect end to our proposal, I don't know what is. I can't wait to be Mrs. Owen Young."

Clapping comes from next door and I turn to see Gordon wheeling himself down the sidewalk. "I think you forgot this, Owen," he says, winking at me. It's a paper that looks like our previous treasure hunt. "The ladies helped me out. Now you can both go searching for the engagement ring."

My heart is full and I'm excited for the future. I get to marry a man who loves me completely and who I absolutely adore. I used to get a bit jealous of my friends in their relationships, but sometimes the best things take time.

The broken road that led me to Owen is a big part of our story, and I can't wait to see what adventures we go on.

"Can we get married at the lake house?" I ask, breathless from kissing no-longer grumpy Owen.

"I wouldn't want it to be anywhere else."

ACKNOWLEDGMENTS

It's been a while since I've done an acknowledgment section, but there are some great people I need to thank. Without them, this book probably wouldn't be finished.

Thanks to Nellie K. Neves for her inspiration for this book. I knew in Matched with Her Athlete Boss that I wanted to have something Evie had to work through, other than relationships. Nellie came through with all the information and scenarios for multiple sclerosis.

Some might wonder why I would do that to one of my characters, but life still happens. And if we can celebrate life in the midst of trials, we're that much better off.

Thank you to Sheree Bingham, who constantly checks on me to make sure I'm reaching my deadlines. I always need that nudge, especially trying to write during the summer.

Thanks to Jordan Truex for proofreading. The comma is my worst skill and thanks for helping me improve on that. As well as being such an avid supporter of authors :)

To Author Kate Watson for helping me tweak and refine this as my beta reader. You're amazing.

To my husband and family, who've survived my early morning writing throughout this summer. Thanks for being my ultimate support system.

And to anyone else I might've forgotten, know that I'll figure it out in the middle of the night :)

ALSO BY BRITNEY M. MILLS

Love in a Snapshot

Love in the Details

Rosemont High Baseball

The Perfect Play

The Perfect Game

The Perfect Catch

The Perfect Steal

The Perfect Hit

Sage Creek Small Town Series

Loving His Flower Shop Girl

Loving His Reporter Girl

Subscribe to the newsletter to get updates on books coming out, cover reveals and the opportunity for giveaways!

ABOUT THE AUTHOR

By day, Britney M. Mills is the wife to a builder and mom to five, but by night, she turns into an author, writing YA & contemporary romance stories.

A book lover, former college athlete, and Jane Austen fan, she crafts stories with the idea that anyone can find love.

When she's not writing, she spends time playing games with her kids, or shuttling them to and from their activities, watching Sanditon and Murdock Mysteries, or dreaming of future characters while she folds a mountain of laundry.

Subscribe to Britney's newsletter for updates, behind-the-scenes and a free book to dive into today!